Get Rich or Try Dying (Part One)

Book 1 in the *Ruthless Mortals'* saga

Raef Mazer

DEDICATION

For all the lost souls, never give up hope.

DISCLAIMER

The story events, characters and organizations are entirely fictional and any similarity between them and any real events, people or organizations are purely coincidental.

Contents

Act 1: Wipeout
Chapter One

Paris 1977

Do you want to know what the seven secrets to world domination are? I know them. These seven pillars of prosperity took me most of my lifetime to discover. I used them to become one of the richest and most powerful people on the planet. Now I will share my hard-won secrets with you.

My name is Henri Jones. I was not always successful. I am not from rich or prodigious parents. I am not strikingly handsome, excessively tall and I lack many of the other attributes that the general population sometimes associate with high achievers.

The truth is that rich people are ugly.

Not all of them but most of them.

I don't mean that rich people are ugly on the outside, especially not the celebrities. Even the *regular* rich lavish time and attention on their clothing, appearance and … let's face it, sometimes they spend a lot of money on gathering together very physically attractive companions. Nevertheless, these wealthy people are usually ugly on the inside.

You might be able to name a lot of super-rich people who seem to have beautiful personalities, but I can guarantee that they each have a legion of PR personnel working hard on that image.

Do you think it is a coincidence that every rich person in the public eye is associated with charitable work?

What about the ones doing serious jail time? Go ahead and Google someone wealthy who is in prison, together with the word *'charity'* and I guarantee the discordant picture of who they are and who they claim to be is plain to see.

You may have seen a cliché image of someone wealthy, throwing money around in a supercar like it was confetti paid for by someone else at a wedding. The reality is that rich people did not get rich by throwing money away.

You might be thinking; *What about the philanthropists?*

The thing about philanthropy is that it costs money.

Acquiring money in the first place requires distinctly non-philanthropic actions.

Robin Hood might have been the most honest philanthropist of them all. After all, at least he openly robbed from the rich and swiftly gave it all to the poor. But then again, Robin Hood was a made-up myth.

Real philanthropists take from everyone they can and then, after some considerable time, give a small amount back to the super-poor. They take the cream from their ill-gotten gains and then throw back some of the leftovers. They let others feed from their scraps and expect some benefit from their actions; gratitude, recognition, a better after-life or perhaps a place in history.

Where *you see* a library named after somebody, *I see* a clever, ruthless and successful egotist.

How do the affluent achieve wealth in abundance? As it turns out, the Robin Hood approach of stealing exclusively from the rich is hard to do successfully and repeatedly. It is much easier to take from everybody without any discrimination at all – and that might be get rich rule number 1:

Never discriminate. Take from as many people as possible – and that is always easier to do when you are perceived to be a giver.

If you have ever worked out how to consistently win at the board game *Monopoly*, you will already know it is about acquiring everything you can as early as possible in the game. Mortgage properties if you have to but be sure to buy everything you land on. Then whoever converts his or her position to a Monopoly first, wins.

Ironically, this game was first intended to be a means to educate people about the evils of unscrupulous wealth and privilege. That was not what it taught me. It taught me that achieving unscrupulous wealth and privilege without showing any generosity or acquiescence is the only way to win.

The game of Monopoly also relies on a degree of chance. The rules of engagement in a board game are set, extremely limited and difficult to cheat without getting caught. The rules of society are different, far more complex than any board game.

The rules of society are easier to navigate and manipulate… if you know how to bend, break or avoid them.

As my story begins, I don't think I was at all ugly on the inside. I was a giver. A giver raised for some of my formative early years in Paris.

Give your mum a kiss.

Give your dad his beer.

It was the mid-seventies. A time when, based on observing my French mother at her waitressing job, old men groping the bottoms of young women as they served food was still considered an unofficial part of the dining experience. Although, the cannier waitresses would often follow-up with an accidental spillage of boiling hot soup into the lap of the offending person, together with a seemingly heartfelt but completely faux apology; *"Oh, Monsieur. Je suis vraiment désolé."* (Oh sir. I am genuinely sorry.)

Fortunately, my mother was never the youngest or most svelte waitress in the room and her bottom was always passed up for her more youthful competition.

I was originally one of a set of two identical twins. Xavier, my brother, was accidentally smothered when

I was two years old. We had shared a bed and it seemed that I might have accidentally suffocated him.

I cannot recall anything from that age, so I had no idea what really happened.

When I was seven, my mother ran off with the local bar owner and left me in Paris with my British father.

Emile, her new beau, was a tubby, grubby, smelly man with a beard like someone had dragged some old wire-wool through a used ashtray. He had breath that smelt like farts. I know that because before my mother left, she used to take me to his bar. I recall that getting close to his face was just like accidently leaning too close to the bowl in a public toilet cubicle when you lean across to flush.

Emile drank a lot of red wine and smoked continuously. His perpetual drinking and smoking made it impossible to tell whether he worked all of the time or none of it.

Given how physically and functionally unappealing Emile was, and that my mother considered him a step-up from dad, you can imagine what kind of person my father was.

Dear old dad also spent little time sober, but unlike Emile, dad deeply enjoyed thumping things. This was probably the reason Emile ran away with mum.

No alcohol support group ever managed to persuade him to give up his personal oasis of twenty-four-hour complimentary wine, but the fear of dad thumping him extremely hard seemed to work just fine.

After mum left, I did my best to self-parent. Not an easy task when you are seven, but I learnt how to intercept some of dad's wages to get some food for the cupboard in the small apartment we lived in. I befriended dad when he was sober and hid from him when he was drunk… which was most of the time.

He told me, *"Drinking helps me with my work."* Dad worked as a truck driver.

From my own observations of Parisienne driving, I was firmly of the belief that most French drivers of the time were applying the same strategy.

In Paris, I would walk past car accidents as often as most people now walk past a Starbucks. It taught me a lot of very colourful French profanities, especially about what one driver may or may not have done to the mother of the other driver.

It would be reasonable to state that I was not a normal child. I found it hard to be natural around other people. They liked it when kids smiled and laughed and my naturally impassive, neutral expression and tendency to stare at fixed positions for lengthy periods of time seemed to unnerve people.

"Stop staring like a cat," my mother used to say. Maybe that's why she left me behind?

I practiced smiling and laughing in the mirror as much as I could. Once I had this skill in hand in private, I tried it out in public, being careful to look for acceptable social cues for when it should happen.

It was an immediate hit.

"*Regarde ça. Henri est normal*" they would say. (Look at that, Henri is normal).

After mum had fled with Emile, I tried befriending as many other kids as I could and found as many places as possible to sleep, hide or hang out when dad was getting feisty and fisty. He might be violent, but he was also lazy and dull-witted. He would never expend more than a token effort looking for me and that reduced my beatings considerably.

Nevertheless, I spent most of the time with a black eye on one or other side of my face.

Fortuitously, less than one year later, at the age of eight, my dad passed away after falling in front of a metro train whilst drunk. It was no great mystery for the French police, the Gendarme, to solve. He was, after all, what the Brits might refer to as an *accomplished and inveterate inebriate.*

Nobody saw him die, but they found him on the tracks and assumed he had either slipped off the platform or maybe jumped down.

There was no funeral. Moreover, I don't think there was anything to show for his life. No assets. Just a tiny apartment with hardly anything in it, except me.

As my mother could not be located, the French authorities sent me over to my paternal grandmother in the UK, to a town on the English Channel called Folkestone.

Chapter Two

Folkestone was a once-glamorous Victorian sea-resort that had not only seen better days but also better decades.

The main street in the town centre had been built at just the wrong orientation so that it entirely missed the sun for all but thirty-minutes at the peak of the day.

When I first arrived, there was an art-deco Lido by the beach. It was demolished and replaced with an asphalt car park.

That was the story of Folkestone, a place that should have had everything but was ostensibly let down by stupid decisions, especially in the area of planning.

The population of the town in the late seventies was a mixed bag. There were still areas of affluence and areas that approached slum conditions.

Grandma lived in one of the poorest and roughest parts of the town, just on the wrong side of the central train station. It was a road full of one-room bedsits, druggies and thugs, interlaced with old folks who still owned full properties. The older residents were mostly a hangover from the nineteen-forties, fifties and sixties.

As dad was a Brit who could speak nearly no French at all, I was already bilingual, but most of my conversations had not been with dad, so I had the misfortune of initially having a French accent. Not that having a French accent is a misfortune of itself, indeed, these days I always use the French accent for public appearances. It was simply that using it could attract the wrong type of attention in the rougher parts of town.

This was further exacerbated by Grandma. She had been an actress in her day. Not a well-known one, but she had that British upper-class BBC accent popular, at that time, among thespians.

I quickly worked out that the accent Grandma was training me to use was a fast-track to getting kicked in. Using pronunciation in public such as "a rind" when you meant "around," "pounds" instead of "quid" or phrases like "I'm terribly sorry" in place of "Oy" accompanied by a menacing stare was not the best way to blend in.

Avoiding being punched-in by bullies on the way home turned out to be quite de rigueur.

I didn't feel comfortable fighting. As with so many social interactions, I was not really sure where the boundaries were.

Was there some sort of ethical boundary about interacting with somebody who had leapt out and started punching you?

Despite being an Anglo-French kid, initially with what some might have called a weird accent, I managed to mostly avoid the junior despots. It was typically easy to outwit them because they came from similar stock; people who had only ever managed to conquer the dizzying heights of being a truck-driver, a benefits claimant, or a convicted thief.

There were no MENSA candidates among them.

Sometimes I would wonder why I was so different from my parents. Had one of them been a secret genius? After all, my own roots seemed to be the same as the other kids – but my way of looking and analysing things seemed entirely different.

Grandma, in common with much of our street, was a benefit claimant. She owned the house but had pretty much nothing else in the coffers and therefore lived from state benefits. The house was run-down, and repairs were only ever performed when they were free, state-provided or had become just beyond essential.

Grandma, as it turned out, was both eccentric and egocentric. She was in her late fifties and fond of fashion…or I should say she was fond of what she considered to be fashion. Think mid-nineteen-thirties style, with the gaudier end of sixties vibrant colours and you are probably in the right ballpark.

She spent a lot of money on the clothes and food she liked.

She bought *my* clothes from second-hand stores and markets.

In every photo of the time, I look like the disgruntled, Dickensian street-urchin who just took a bath after getting out of a chimney.

Expensive hairdos for granny. A pudding bowl haircut for me.

Fish for granny and slightly out-of-date, cheap fish fingers for me.

"You know fish don't actually have fingers." I would

complain, especially when they tasted like fish poo.

I would regard the labels in my school uniform with discomfort. They often had the names of other kids I was at school with, stuff they had thrown out and now I was expected to wear. Generally, these were items of clothing cast aside for good reason. Poison-white shirts, worn out jumpers covered with bobbles and hanging threads…

On the bright side, Granny was not punchy like her son was. She was just totally self-absorbed and slightly poor.

Whereas most of the other kids seemed to have two parents and enough money to clothe them well, I was the exact opposite – and there were literally no other kids like me at my school.

However, I did have one redeeming feature. It transpired that I was significantly smarter than any of my classmates. I might have been bottom of the class in terms of appearance, but I was top of the class in anything and everything academic – much to the chagrin of some of the teachers.

In the school sponsored spell, I was one of only five students who scored one hundred out of one hundred, and the only one aged under ten. Sadly, for the school, I didn't actually have any sponsorship money for my achievement. That seemed to annoy the head teacher, Mr Canning, because he mentioned the other four people in morning assembly to rapturous applause and then mumbled my first name under his breath afterwards like my result didn't really count, or as though I had cheated.

Of course, sport is not an academic subject – and I was not at all good at that. My stature was somewhat shorter and leaner than the school athletes. Even if I had been stockier, I believe my nineteen-fifties flared shorts would have created enough aerodynamic drag to lose every race.

My swim apparel was also dated. As I tried to explain to Grandma, generally swimming trunks in the seventies don't have built-in belts. As far as I could tell, belts in swimming trunks were phased out sometime in the early sixties. Possibly even the eighteen-sixties.

Apparently, those were the only type of swimming trunks in my size Grandma had been able to find in the local charity stores. Nobody was throwing out speedos.

Worse still, I didn't get laughed at by the other kids at the swimming lessons. It was more like they felt sorry for me. I didn't like that.

It was at the first school sports day I attended when things went further downhill. To me, this seemed to be a day that was about showing that winning really did matter.

I was still just eight-years-old at this point. We all had to take our little chairs out to the playing field. We filed down through the playground, where I tripped and fell, knocking all of my front teeth on to the back of the chair and into a crooked mess.

There was no fear of expensive dentistry looming. After all, this was the UK, a country almost unscathed by the science of modern dentistry – and frankly Granny couldn't give a fig. She certainly wasn't going to part with any of the money she didn't have to get my teeth back in order.

"Ah, never mind," is what she said when I got home with a bloody rag pressed to my mouth. She hadn't come to see the sports day, which in my opinion was a good thing.

Rounding out my ragamuffin look was now a smile that looked like it belonged on a Picasso.

"One day," Granny would say, *"you will be able to earn your own money — and then you can buy whatever you like."*

According to the law of the time, it seemed that I needed to reach the age of about fourteen to really start earning my own money.

I couldn't wait.

Chapter Three

After ten months of settling in with Grandma. It finally happened.

I got beaten up in the UK for the first time.

It was an interesting experience and not half as bad as I thought it would be.

I did not fight back. I just studied what was happening. It was only one kid, and he was not particularly good at it. Not like dad had been. He ran up on me from behind. It hardly hurt at all. Some cuts and grazes from the punching, bruises from the belly kicks and a swollen eye.

Granny was mortified. That surprised me, since, from her lack of concern about my clothing and disfigured front teeth, I didn't think she cared about my appearance. She asked who it was – but I didn't tell her.

That week, I did look at all the fight moves on the cop shows of the time. Perhaps I could pick up some useful moves? Generally, these shows featured homicides and punch-ups. I managed to watch one Bruce Lee martial arts film which was more promising.

A few weeks later, once the cuts had nearly healed, the same kid jumped me again. This time he lay in wait, pressed against the wall of a side alley.

On this occasion, he had a friend that he was aiming to impress. At least I think that was what it was, since the friend just stood there dumbfounded.

The bully, *Daz* was his name, jumped out and started punching and kicking randomly. I moved my back to him, placed my hand over my fist and powered my elbow back into his stomach.

There was a satisfying grunt as he doubled over. I pushed him to the ground and started kicking him really hard in the stomach and ribs.

His friend stood there, jaw open and finally said. "Well, that doesn't look like any fun at all." With that, his friend just walked off.

The bully lay there in the street, crying. It was probably enough. I had nothing to be gained by continuing, so I followed the other boy down the street.

A few interesting things happened the next day. The most interesting was that the boy that had tried to beat me up twice attempted to make friends with me. And they think that *I* am strange?

The other unusual event was that the kid he had been with had gone missing. It was the seventies; it could have been any number of strange men. This was the era of stranger danger.

They found his body a few days later, he seemed to have choked on a plastic bag and fallen into a river. It was incredibly sad. That was what my grandmother said.

Chapter Four

It had become clear early on that grandma was a lousy cook. It was not just the ingredients that were below par. Everything was burnt within an inch of edibility.

Her eyesight was poor and despite her attention to personal appearance and personal cleanliness, the house itself was kept like a hoarder's midden.

Low value artefacts from broken pots to beaten-up books were piled high in the hallway, landings and most rooms. Even the bathroom looked like a museum of shabby, defunct and out-of-date toiletries.

It was advisable for me to tackle the washing-up regularly to avoid the chances of encountering the remnants of several previous meals when eating.

The house was cold all-year round. That was great in the summer but decidedly uncomfortable in the winter. It was normal to wake up on harsh mornings to the sight of my own breath in the air and a shallow layer of ice on the inside of my bedroom window.

The main form of heating in the house were the cats. There were over two dozen of them at any one time. Grandma would take a hot water bottle and just about all of them to bed with her each evening.

I was allergic to cats. That is what the doctor told Grandma; He said, "They are the reason that he sneezes and scratches." But as Grandma explained to the doctor; the cats were there first and she preferred them. She could get rid of me if the doctor thought that might fix the problem?

The doctor did not look in the least bit amused and I just looked as indifferent as ever.

I would have got rid of the cats, but more than twenty cats going missing at once was implausible and besides, she would have replaced them within a matter of days.

I kept my bedroom door shut and that at least reduced my symptoms, although it was close to impossible to make it through the house, in any direction, without becoming a mass transit vehicle for the fleas.

Aside from the cats, my other pressing concern became a school exam.

In that particular region of the UK, they still ran a system known as *selective education*. This meant that the brightest children were identified through a single academic test and had the opportunity of going to schools that would theoretically optimise the academic achievements of their students.

This test was known as the *eleven plus* exam, as it would determine which school was most suitable after you turned eleven years of age.

The exam was a doddle. I was struck by how stupid some children must be when examples of the questions included a drawing of a tree and four choices to tick; Was it (a) a fridge, (b) a rainbow, (c) a tree or (d) a power station?

The results were kept secret, insofar as you only

found out if you had passed or not. My alleged result was therefore a surprise. Apparently, I was *borderline*. I had never heard of that outcome before. Everyone either *passed* or *failed*.

How could I not have sailed through the test with a blistering passing grade? There had not been a single question with which I had struggled.

This made no sense.

Grandma would discuss the result a lot with her friends, and I would surreptitiously eavesdrop from outside the lounge. The most likely theory it seemed was that I had been branded as a throwaway child from a low-income household; that the powers that be had decided to keep me out of the elite.

"They don't want a parentless grandchild from a spinster in the rough end of town in the grammar school." That is what Aunt Sylvia had said to grandma.

Was this really true?

Aunt Sylvia was sure of it and in an act of kindness, paid for me to get independently intelligence tested by a child psychologist. Something that I understood cost her well over £100, no small amount back then.

Aunt Sylvia was not a real aunt. Grandma and I had no other family. Sylvia was a good friend of grandma, and I was taught that all of her friends should be called *aunt* this or *uncle* that.

In the meantime, it was also determined that my early September birth date meant I should be held back a year before attending high school, or 'secondary school' as it is known in the UK.

This was a dreadful turn of events. I was already top of the class and repeating a year of primary school while my classmates did not, was something that annoyed me.

A few months later I was taken up to London and sat down to a set of tests that were considerably more difficult than the eleven-plus.

Complex patterns and number sequences to solve. Substantial mathematical equations. Spelling and grammatical errors to identify.

I was told I would have two tests. Each would run for 45 minutes. One on math's and one on English. I was not required to complete all the questions; it was only important to do the best I could.

I finished the math's and patterns paper with a couple of minutes to spare. I got close to completing the English paper, but I ran out of time a few questions from the end.

To my surprise, after the tests, we were told to wait in the reception area. An hour later, Grandma and I were given some of the results.

"It's good news," said the psychologist. "He aced the tests."

According to the results, at age eleven as I was by then, I had the English language ability of at least sixteen and my math's score was 100%, meaning that I had the math's ability of at least eighteen.

"In other words, Ms Jones," said the psychologist, "not only can you insist on sending him to the grammar school of your choice, but you can even insist that he skip a year."

It was at that point that the psychologist asked to see Grandma on her own and I was asked to sit out in the unmanned reception area. I went and sat down as I had been asked and as soon as the door was closed, moved back to the door and pressed my ear against it.

I couldn't hear everything clearly, but there were some questions to Grandma. *Did I have any friends? Was I always prone to being so introvert and expressionless?*

When they walked to the door, I scurried back to my seat, grabbed a magazine from the coffee table and did my best to look nonchalant. I was called back in. I threw the copy of what turned out to be *Knitting Monthly* back on the coffee table and did my best to put on lots of smiley expressions and talk a bit about the people at school.

The question was then put to me.

Did I want to skip a year?

Not really. *What I would really like is for whoever tried to do me over to regret doing it.* Naturally, I did not say that part aloud.

It must have been Mr Canning, the primary school headteacher. I was sure of it. He never liked me. He was a Christian traditionalist and some scruffy, parentless, wonky-toothed, belt-trunked, French half-breed taking the place of someone more normal must have been a step too far for him.

It was clear to me that I needed to spend a lot more time in the coming months understanding how people work. I was particularly interested in how criminals work. What motivates them and how they operate?

Grandma had plenty of books about murder, but the thing about books on murder is that they only get written when people get caught.

I didn't need to know about people who got caught. I needed to find out about the people that didn't get caught.

The best way of doing that would be to somehow get close to a police officer.

With little effort, I was able to identify that Carl Ross, a kid in my year had a dad who was a policeman. I was usually quite a loner, but against my normal nature, I set about making Carl my best friend.

I also joined the local library.

Chapter Five

Perhaps you have never thought too much about avenging the wrongs that people do to you. That is quite usual. The world is full of people that take no counteraction against those that have harmed them.

Forgiveness is something I have never understood. To me, forgiveness seems to be a form of acquiescence, acceptance without protest.

But even the word *protest* is weak. When a child protests, it is generally ignored. But when a child does something wrong, it is generally forgiven. And when a child does something completely unthinkable, the kid is not usually even a suspect.

It was not that I wanted revenge on Mr Canning. I just wanted to ensure he could do nothing more to ruin my life. I felt he was unworthy of having any power in this world and that I had the ability to change that.

Although Mr Canning vaunted himself as a Christian, in truth he seemed to think of himself more as a hand of God than as a servant.

Major Canning, as he liked to be called, was pious, sexist, aspiring middle-class and like most men of his age, ex-military, having served in the British army during World War II.

Mr Canning insisted on being called Major Canning, so I always took delight in calling him Mr Canning. It would not have surprised me if it turned out that he had in fact fought for the SS division of the Nazis, although, according to him he had been one of the first ever British commandos.

Canning liked caning naughty boys and treating his female staff like second-rate infantrymen. His Mark II Ford Escort was his pride and joy; a car which arrived like clockwork at 07:45 each morning and left at exactly 18:15 each evening.

You might be wondering; *How did I know Canning was a sexist?*

Grandma had told me a lot about how almost all men are sexist and had mentioned this was especially true of Mr Canning. Indeed, Mr Canning showed he was a sexist at a brief special education lesson in my final year at primary school. The boys and girls had been split into two groups to talk about the birds and the bees. It was all quite vague really.

I guess the girls were being told about things like periods, things I had no knowledge of at that age.

The boys were given a very flimsy description of sex. How when a man and a woman love each other – the man can put a seed inside the woman's tummy.

Biologically, the initial story Mr Canning told was a mess, if not thoroughly inaccurate.

Fortunately, Mrs Waverley, the school secretary was present and had some diagrammatic handouts of the male and female *bits*. Much hilarity ensued as everyone was asked if they each had both a penis and a vagina. Billy had several penises and no vagina, some people had neither – but eventually every boy had one of each.

One point the Major was keen to make was this; "When you marry, it is essential that the woman is still a virgin." That meant that no man had ever tried to put a seed in her tummy.

On the other hand, when Billy asked if that meant Mr Canning was a virgin when he was married, he was emphatic; "Oh no. I served in the army. It's not important for the man to be a virgin. Men need to be more adventurous than women."

There was a certain lack of logic to his story. I can also recall thinking; *Who on Earth thought this guy would be great at shaping the minds of young children?*

At the end of the lesson, I folded my penis and vagina and placed them both in my pocket. I would study them more later.

Chapter Six

My abject poverty hung heavily on my mind. By this time, I had turned my room into a small sanctuary of tidiness. It was not possible for my room to be full of nice things, or new things, but they could at least be full of clean and tidy things.

Sheets and shirts of poison-white could not be un-poisoned, but they could at least be as clean as possible.

The threadbare carpet was still threadbare, but regularly vacuumed by me and now dust-free. I had raided the house for any useful items and found very few, except for some of Grandma's true crime books and an old, empty Polaroid camera I had picked-up for ten pence from a jumble sale.

The polaroid camera was a bargain, so I thought. Until I found out that the film would cost over £3 just for a cartridge of ten pictures.

I had managed to acquire a second-hand black and white portable tv, sporting a huge twelve-inch screen and picking up the three television channels that were available at the time. Grandma didn't believe in the excesses of colour television because of the cost, so she said. I think the real reason was that she was colour-blind, which could easily explain some of the amazingly uncoordinated outfits she wore.

It didn't matter. TV was dull anyway and rarely had any content about how to make money.

I did not want to wait until I was fourteen to start earning, so I set about asking how other people made money.

During the summer months, Folkestone beach would be littered with holidaymakers. Dotted along the beach in a few locations were various kiosks selling ice-creams and frozen lollies.

I hit upon a plan. By this time, I had managed to save a couple of pounds in coins. I would buy a cheap multi-pack of choc-ices from the supermarket in town and sell them to the people on the beach.

I researched my market. The kiosks had a start price of ten pence for their smallest ice-lollies and twenty-five pence for their choc-ices. I could get a twelve pack of cheap choc-ices for £1 and sell them directly on the beach for twenty pence each.

I had just reached the magical savings number of £3, which I had intended to spend on film for the camera. Instead, I decided to go all in and buy three packs of the choc-ices. I would have to move the stock fast to prevent the merchandise from melting.

"Choc-ices, 20p each. Six for a pound." That was what I said as I weaved through the towels and holidaymakers on the beach. By this time, I could lose all trace of my original French accent and sound like a proper, British-born, Kentish, lower-class market trader by replacing terms such as *"Hello there, it's nice to meet you."* With the more colloquial greeting of *"Alwight mate?"*

It was a sweltering day, and it did not take long for the stock to sell out.

It was still hot, so I headed back up the cliffs and into town. I now had £6.80. This time I purchased six packs of twelve individually wrapped, budget choc-ices and headed back down to the beach.

I was about half-way through my second stint when a man grabbed me by the ear. It turned out he was the owner of several of the beach kiosks. He told me it was illegal for me to sell my choc-ices and that he could report me to the police. He said that I should run off and never come back.

I told him my friend was in the police and he let go of my ear. He told me to "Hoppit," and I duly did. Although I did sell all but the final pack on the way off the beach, to a shout of "Oy" from the kiosk-owner.

As I left the beach eating one of the final choc-ices, I found a man lying underneath the front of a car. His family stood around as he worked.

I offered them an ice-cream each. These ones were now a bit melted, so I let them have them at cost-price.

What was the man doing? He was a mechanic. He was fixing a brake problem.

I was interested. *How did he know he had a brake problem and how was he going to fix it?* I noticed he too drove a Ford Escort, albeit an older model than Mr Canning's.

When his family had returned to the car from the beach, there had been a dark fluid on the ground. The mechanic had investigated and found the brake pipe had become loose. He showed me how the pipes ran, where the bleed valve was. It was all remarkably interesting.

I thanked them very much and headed home.

I now had £10.70 and a slight spring in my step.

A few days later, the headline in the local newspaper read; *Ice-Cream Kiosks Vandalised by Arsonists*.

These were the happy days before CCTV was a thing. The police had nothing much to go on and Carl's dad confirmed this. Although the owner had spotted some young kid of perhaps seven or eight years of age, so he thought, selling ice-creams on the beach.

I was ten, it couldn't possibly have been me. Besides, I had not told anyone about my beach enterprise. I had no-one I wanted to tell.

Nobody thought it could be the young kid anyway, after all, it happened in the early hours of the morning. What kind of child would be out unnoticed at that time?

A child living with an elderly relative in a big house would be my guess. Especially if the elderly relative slept at the very top of the house and the child did not.

My intention when burning down the kiosks had been to create a monopoly on the beach. It looked like that was no longer a viable plan.

That is get rich rule number 2:

To earn supernormal profit, you must dominate your market and create a monopoly as early as you can.

Chapter Seven

The following Tuesday, just three weeks before the school term ended, Mr Canning fell dreadfully ill. According to what I overheard, he had been sweating profusely, then started vomiting, struggling for breath and becoming confused.

In the end they had to call an ambulance.

There was quite a commotion. Everybody's attention focused on Mr Canning as he was stretchered out of the building. This distraction allowed me to slip unnoticed into his office.

He didn't die or anything.

Some people thought it was a dodgy school meal. I thought it was more likely that *someone* had managed to mix a small amount of deadly nightshade into his gravy when the canteen staff were preparing his dinner tray.

I had to be careful with the dose. Just a few berries more and he would have died. If he died, according to the true-crime books, there would be an enquiry and an autopsy. I needed to avoid that.

He had to be off work on sick leave for the rest of the week.

During that time, there was a further commotion. The school invited Grandma and I to see Mrs Findlay, the Deputy Head.

Apparently, during the headteachers sick leave some polaroid photos of a young boy had been found in Mr Canning's office. They appeared to be shot in his office and show a small boy in a certain state of undress. Although they didn't show the face of the boy, there was a rather distinguishing swimming trunk belt in view. *Did I know anything about it?*

Too flaming right, I did; I had been practicing this part for ages.

I broke down in tears. *They were only pictures. He had wanted me to do other stuff, but I had refused. It all happened last year. He told me that if I refused, he would make sure I didn't get into any of the good secondary schools. But I had refused, nonetheless.*

Now we would find out if Mr Canning had been to blame for manipulating my eleven-plus outcome. The police were called.

I had not expected to be grilled myself, but grilled I was. This was a serious accusation, so they thought. But as I pointed out it was only photographs. Nothing else happened.

As it turned out, Mr Canning *had* interfered with my next choice of school. What excuse could he use? Prejudice? It sounded lame.

Unexpectedly, two other boys came forward with revelations about Mr Canning. It seemed that I had inadvertently done something good. Perhaps I was a hero?

Canning was allowed back to school only to collect his car and even then, the school Governors insisted that he was escorted at all times when on the property and not allowed to see any of the kids.

He must have been quite depressed, because on his way home he crashed his car into a wall. I was told that he was quite severely injured and now walks with a limp.

He said the brakes failed but there was not much left of the car and certainly no evidence of brake fluid loss where it had been parked. I was sure there was no evidence.

Happy days.

A further unexpected outcome from Mr Canning's early retirement is that I and some of the other boys had to go for a series of psychological counselling sessions.

This was a lesson for me. I should always try to avoid any direct involvement in my exploits. At a minimum, I should avoid being caught up in the aftermath.

How did I feel about what Mr Canning had done to me?

How did I feel about anything?

It was not that I had no feelings at all, it was simply like they were on a really, really low volume setting.

I was not about to reveal that to any counsellor.

What I did instead was to tap into my muted emotions about being done over on my choice of schools. *It was very upsetting* I had said, *but at least everything had turned out well in the end.*

With secondary school looming and far too much attention focused on how the events may have psychologically damaged me, I decided that I needed to portray the persona of a consummate saint.

Carl, my one friend, was also going to the same secondary school as I was. It was an all-boys school.

His dad had been particularly helpful in deflecting any suspicion from me during the Mr Canning incident. Sure, the police had given me a grilling, but they had also been assuaged by Detective Constable Ross. His character assessment of me was that I was a good boy.

Mr Canning had been at great pains to point out that he had no polaroid camera. *Did I have a polaroid camera?* No, I did not. Such things were surely expensive, and I could not even afford a decent school uniform.

They did check my room but found no camera.

If they fingerprinted the polaroid's, they would have found nothing on them at all. My research into crimes had served me well. Each film was sealed inside a cartridge, all I had to do was be sure not to touch them with my bare hand as they emerged from the camera.

The true crimes book was already back in the general mess of Grandma's midden.

With the revelations from some of the other boys, Detective Ross and the other police involved threw the book at Mr Canning. They did not like what they referred to as "kiddy-fiddlers," especially when their own children could have been at risk.

Chapter Eight

The bad news was that I continued to be poor. I had £7.40 to my name after paying for the polaroid film. Grandma gave me just fifty pence per week pocket-money.

I turned my hand to washing cars at fifty pence a time, but in my neighbourhood, most people either did not wash their cars at all or were so obsessed with polishing them that they would never trust that task to my second-rate cleaning set-up.

After six weeks of the summer break, I had only managed to wash twenty cars, bringing in a meagre £10. Worst of all, it was hard work, with no possibility of making any serious money.

Some days, Carl and I would go down to the amusement arcades on the seafront. I never took any money with me. I waited until some of the push machines dropped money when unattended, then reinvested that into other push machines where the money looked as though it was on the brink of falling into the winnings tray.

That rarely yielded more than one or two pounds on a good day and flat zero on most days. The only person that really made money in the arcades was the owner.

By the end of the summer, less my expenditure on sweets I had amassed the sum of £23.67. Even I knew that was not great. I had friends who got more than that from distant relatives on their birthday.

My own birthday fell just a few days before I started at my new school.

Grandma's presents were always disappointing. They would typically be some item of rubbish from a charity store and be in some or other way defective or substandard; Jigsaws with missing pieces, a stereo with a broken cassette deck and a broken stylus on the record deck, a bike with just one gear.

About the best present I ever got was new shoes.

It was now 1982 and I was approaching my twelfth birthday, Grandma proudly announced that she had really spent a lot on me for once. She did not say what she had purchased, only that it had cost nearly £130.

For grandma to spend £130 on me was an unprecedented event. *"It's an investment in your future."*

I had been dropping some mighty hints about getting a home computer. Specifically, a Sinclair ZX Spectrum. £130 was exactly what they cost at the time. I speculated this with Carl who was fired up and ready to come around the following evening.

As far as I could see, computers were going to be the magical money-makers of the future. Logically, there was nothing else the old bat could have purchased.

I awoke on the morning of my birthday to find Grandma beaming over a large box which was wrapped quite badly on all sides except the base.

I rarely felt much emotion but seeing the size of that box I felt what I think would be described as wholesale disappointment, coupled with a light amount of anger.

The box was too large to be the specific home computer I had asked for. *Perhaps she had purchased the much bulkier and far less useful BBC model B computer for me?* The box was the right size for that but surely that would be more expensive than the £130 Grandma had mentioned.

I placed my hands on the box and my disappointment deepened. Through the wrapping paper, I could feel some kind of textured wood. As far as I knew, there was no computer on Earth that came supplied in a wooden box.

I pulled the paper up and off the box.

It was an old wooden box with two hinges.

"It's a piano accordion." Said Grandma excitedly.

I was dumbstruck. *What the fire truck?* That's what I thought.

I had never expressed interest in any musical instrument, and I certainly did not need any further drains on my already lack-lustre credibility.

"Oh look, here comes Henri with his piano accordion." This was not the kind of statement I could imagine any of my future classmates making with any kind of positive inflection.

I was still incredibly short for my age. It took both grandma and I to lift the accordion on to the dining room table. She held one end and I pulled the other, then pushed it.

It made a tuneless wheeze that reminded me of the tramps and buskers along the River Seine.

"Thanks." I said, not really hiding my disgust.

"You can make a lot of money playing a musical instrument." Grandma said encouragingly.

This was doubtful for any instrument, but to my mind I had never heard of a superstar piano accordion player with a recording contract. Besides which, it would take me several years before I could even lift it without help. It was more like a portable church organ and must have weighed close to thirty pounds.

I needed to cancel the plans to play with Carl tonight.

Aunt Sylvia had got me a £5 book token from WH Smiths; *'It's like real money but you can only spend it on books."*

So not like real money at all then.

The house needed more books like a sinking hot air balloon needs more ballast.

Had she not heard about libraries?

Chapter Nine

I kept a low profile at my new school. I made neither friends nor enemies. I hung about with Carl sometimes, but he mostly spent his time with new friends, playing football.

My second-hand, off-trend school uniform and free school meals continued to mark me out from the other students who almost exclusively it seemed came from families with money.

Being in an all-boys environment was, I had guessed, a bit like visiting an all-male prison each day.

Firstly, everywhere smelt like sweaty gym socks and dirty underpants. Everywhere, that was, except the gym. In the gym, you had to try and hold your breath until you could exit.

Only one place smelt worse: the school bus.

It was like Satan himself had commissioned the vehicle; grouchy driver, floor and seats that had never been cleaned, the stench of rotting packed lunch remnants and the smell of seventy boys packed together with standing room only.

The school building mostly dated from the late 19th century; huge doors, large wooden windows, solid wood flooring and stone staircases with enamelled steel railings that would be illegal by any modern health and safety standards.

It was an environment designed to take the daily knocks from its' students.

Hundreds of boys would gather at the school each day with their collective behaviour not only unchecked by the fairer sex but also positively pushed downhill by the type of teachers, almost all men, who wanted to be in the company of elitist boys.

The passive and active forms of sexism were rife here.

If you were not joining in with laughing about women or jokes about women or lude comments about women, then you must be one – and that was considered an insult.

Unlike the bullying I had witnessed in my youth, the bullying at the selective school was psychological and fashioned entirely out of testosterone. It was fascinating.

Whatever your most distinguishing feature, whether you were short, tall, ugly, fat, skinny, black, Jewish, Chinese, Spanish, French, smelly or as in my case – dressed like a tramp, there were insulting terms for us all.

Casual racism went unchecked and that went double when the staff did it.

The more emotionally upsetting you found name-calling, the more of it you attracted.

As a person with nearly no emotional response, this was excellent news for me. I didn't care much about anything and certainly not somebody shouting "Oy, Hobo" or "stenchy Frenchy" down the corridor. Eventually my insulting nickname became "rag and bones" because it referred to my second-hand appearance, skinny stature and rhymed with Henri Jones.

I was not smelly. I might have been wearing old clothes, but I had become an obsessive compulsive about my cleanliness.

I quite liked this name, especially when it became shortened to "Bones" since he was a character on *Star Trek*.

All of this raw, exaggerated male behaviour was teaching me a lot about people and how to manipulate them.

The people doing the insulting were, it seemed, the ones who lived most in fear of their particular Achille's heel being called out.

Because I gave the insults no heed, aside from occasionally being called *Bones*, they soon disappeared. It was as though the people hurling the insults did not want to waste calories on something that did not work.

That was, however, unwelcome news for the people who were sensitive about something, because it meant that the psychological torment intensified on those that were most impacted by it.

The people driven mad by the insults were caught inside some kind of mental impasse where the obvious need to ignore the insults was unobtainable. They would be wound tighter and tighter every day until they snapped.

Sometimes the snap was an outburst, sometimes it was a fight, sometimes it was crying in a toilet cubicle whilst the nastier end of the school population poured water over you.

For the most part, I failed to excel at the new school and played my part in staying firmly in the middle of class performance. This was intentional. I had worked out that if I appeared to be too bright, I would never get away with anything.

I continued to be bad at sport. Although, I was interested in learning one particular manoeuvre in football. It was against the rules but there was a particularly effective way of fouling a player from behind. It involved gently kicking your opponent's left or right foot with your own when his foot was off the ground and in motion. By kicking the foot sideways so that it hit the back of the calf of the opponent's other leg, he would fall flat on his face, every time.

It was relatively easy to master but after a few too many uses on the playing field, I was told to stop doing it by my classmates.

I did not mind being bad at sport, but one class performance really confused me. I had always thought that my ability in English was exceptionally good. Even the psychologist had said it was. In that first year of high school, regardless of how hard I tried, my scores in English were always graded C, C minus or sometimes even a D.

That score put me firmly at the bottom in that subject.

English was about the only lesson for which my seventh-grade class had a female teacher, Mrs Marsh. She was in her late forties, stocky but not fat and wore make-up that made her look like Coco the Clown; Rich red lipstick, plenty of rouge, a lot of foundation and jet-black hair dye.

It was her first year of teaching at the school and she was not good at it. Mrs Marsh struggled to get the class under control and would usually need to get Mr Copeland, the teacher in the next class along to come in and read each class the riot act.

The school had many forms of discipline open to it at the time.

Detention was a one-hour inconvenience at the end of the day. *An imposition*, as they called it, was a requirement to complete a page or two of lines or write a particular essay. At the top of the heap was a *caning* by the head teacher.

There was one time when Mrs Marsh blew her stack at the class. It appeared she had finally reached her breaking point. Mrs Marsh had never disciplined anyone before. She had never raised her voice before – and this was not just a raised voice yell. She let rip with a banshee style tirade of general abuse, followed by the glowering eye scanning the room for the first person to twitch.

For the first time ever, she brought the class into total silence.

She singled out the ringleader, a boy called Clive Wells and called him to the front of the class.

She pulled out what the entire class considered to be the most heinous and impressive piece of lined paper anyone in the class had ever seen. It was a sheet of paper with lines so narrowly spaced, it looked as though she had it designed by an expert in microfilm. It appeared to contain more real estate than six sides of any normal paper.

All this time when she had looked like a pussycat, had it all been an act?

She finally had control of the class. None of us wanted to write out both sides of a sheet like that.

She looked sternly at Clive and with a slow and steady voice said, *"You are going to take this sheet and write 'I will not speak over the teacher'…"* then a dramatic pause *"…ten times."*

Ten times? The class exploded with laughter. Most of the naughtier children were now raising their hands asking if they could have one too.

By the end of the lesson her short-lived classroom control credibility was in shreds. Clive actually put the ten completed lines on her desk as he left the room.

I had not joined in on any of this behaviour. I was too pre-occupied with my English performance. I felt sure that for some reason, I must have an issue with my English ability because if Mrs Marsh had any grudge or prejudice; how could it be against me?

In the weeks that followed, I got sick. It was some kind of flu that was going around the school.

When I returned to school, I had work to catch up on, including a book review on *The Time Machine*, a book I had missed reading due to my absence.

Mrs Marsh told me to just copy out the work from another boy in the class as catch up.

Jeremy Simpson seemed like a suitable candidate,

he always got straight A's. Doubtless this essay would not be marked because I was just copying it out, but I could at least start to try and understand where my own essays were going wrong.

I duly copied out his *A*-graded book review word-for-word.

We had to hand in our workbooks on a weekly basis. Homework was marked and notes were inspected to ensure we were keeping up.

To my surprise, after handing in my workbook that week, it returned with a grade for the essay I had copied. Marked in large red pen was the letter *F*.

I could not understand it.

I went up to the teacher at the end of the class. Perhaps the *F* was because I had missed the essay?

"Mrs Marsh. I just wanted to ask you about this essay you graded *F*;" …. Before I could say anything more, Mrs Marsh was already going full tilt at the essay.

"It wasn't good at all. Terrible structure. It didn't look like you had even read the book."

After a confused pause, I replied. I reminded Mrs Marsh that this was not my essay, that I had, as instructed, copied out Jeremy's A-graded essay due to my absence.

There was an awkward pause. She took my book from me, scribbled out the *F*, substituted a *C* and then waved me off.

It was suddenly clear to me that I might not have a problem in English per se but more of a problem with the English teacher.

Chapter Ten

Research your market before entering it.

That would be get rich tip number 3.

At this point, I had no idea this was a useful skill for acquiring wealth, but I did know it was an essential ingredient for committing a crime and getting away with it.

I was in the market to decimate the career of yet another teacher. My research identified that Mrs Marsh was, despite her age, in her very first year of teaching.

She was a failed librarian.

How can anyone fail at being a librarian? Surely all you had to be able to do was nail the Dewey decimal system.

She had an assessment coming up. It was going to be an observed lesson. It was only one lesson, and it was with my class.

Having completely ruined her own ability to keep the class in check, I felt confident that she would, left to her own devices, fail the assessment miserably.

I set about circulating various rumours among my classmates.

The day of the assessment arrived.

The observer, a man in his late fifties took a seat at the back of the room and told the class to just completely forget he was present.

Mrs Marsh had not yet arrived, and the class was

in typical, rowdy form. Balls of paper, as well as insults flew through the air, chairs were pushed over.

When the bell went to signify the start of class, Mrs Marsh arrived. I could see she was nervous about the assessment and the specific class involved. She said to the class, in a very timid voice that seemed resigned to failure; "Settle down please."

At that moment, everyone went quiet. All the chairs were put back in place and everyone sat silent and motionless.

Mrs Marsh looked unnerved but began by asking us all to get our current reading book, *Great Expectations*, exercise books and pens out. Everyone did so.

She asked what the class thought about the book so far.

"It's an impressive story." Said Clive Wells.

"Why do you think that?" asked Mrs Marsh, fully expecting this fake veneer to disappear at any time.

"It's the juxtaposition of counter-stereotypes. The person you expect to be good turning out bad and vice-versa."

"Very good." Said Mrs Marsh deftly trying to hide her shock at the class behaviour and the latent intelligence Clive had been hiding from her.

The double-lesson continued this way. Thirty minutes in and we were asked to each write a brief summary of our thoughts on what we had read.

Everyone put their heads down, still in total silence.

By the time the bell sounded for the end of the

lesson. Mrs Marsh had found her stride. We were not arrogant, cruel little boys after all. We knew this was pivotal to her career and we had helped her to ace the observation. How kind.

Everyone filed out of the classroom, leaving Mrs Marsh to the observer. I went down the stairs with the other boys, along the corridor and then back up the second staircase and hung around a dead end of the corridor, pretending to read one of the school noticeboards.

The observer left the room, still congratulating Mrs Marsh on her performance. In truth, I was unsure if she was going to be left on her own, but I figured after such a pivotal moment, she would take time to silently gather herself and wallow in self-relief at what had just happened.

She gathered her books together into her shoulder bag.

The corridor was empty, it was lunchtime, and everyone was downstairs, in the canteen, in the playground or out playing football.

She did not see me when she exited the room and turned left to head downstairs to the staff room. I moved as stealthily as I could; timing would be everything.

There was still nobody else about.

As she reached the very top of the antiquated stone and steel staircase, I crept up behind her and was ready to deftly kick her left foot behind her right calf. That would make her trip flat on her face down the stone staircase with its sharp metal railings.

From what I understood, that might not kill her, but it would certainly be enough to put her out of school for the rest of the year. If she had flunked the assessment, she would still have stayed in the school and the finger of suspicion would be on my classmates and me.

I would not wait around to see the end result. I intended to remain unnoticed. My exit plan was along the upstairs corridor, down the second staircase and straight to the canteen for my free meal.

I hesitated. I put my foot back on the ground and as she took her first step down the staircase, I said "Mrs Marsh."

The shock alone nearly sent her down the stairs because she had no idea I was there.

After clutching her chest momentarily, she said "Yes Henri?"

"Why did you mark my essay unfairly?"

"I didn't..." she trailed off and seemed to be reflecting again on her classroom observation. She paused.

"I think," she said with more confidence," that each one of us has biases and that sometimes we don't recognize them until something happens. I was not aware that I was marking your work unfairly until you copied that essay. It was not intentional. I will be sure to mark your work more equitably in the future and..." she paused again "I'm sorry and thank you for talking to me about this."

Pushing her down the stairs at this point would be amazing. I would have an apology and be able to inflict significant injury. However, she would also know it was me.

I paused.

"Thank you, Mrs Marsh."

She smiled and turned, then proceeded down the staircase.

I followed her down the stairs. It was good of her to apologise. What a weak person she was.

As she turned to go down the second flight of steps, something happened that would change my life. She tripped over. I had nothing to do with it.

There was an audible crunch as she hit the stone staircase.

The ensuing results were an immediate catastrophe. Mrs Marsh had cracked her skull, broken a hip and an arm.

I flagged down a member of staff, Mr Copeland.

What was I doing there with Mrs Marsh? "Just discussing schoolwork." I had said.

Had I pushed Mrs Marsh down the stairs? She could not say one way or the other. Due to the concussion, the event itself was a blur. One thing she was certain of, I had waited around after class and challenged her marking of my work.

It certainly had been my intention to push her down the stairs, but I hadn't. That is not what I said. I told the school clearly that I had not pushed her down the stairs, which was true.

There was a reason there was no physical bullying at this school. They had no tolerance for that sort of behaviour. They also had no tolerance for anything they reasonably suspected to be an attempt at physical bullying, especially against teachers.

I was forced to explain the reason I had challenged her. The unfairly graded essay. I thought this would be my excuse but instead the school saw it as a clear motive.

I was not caned, I was sent straight home and the following day, the school telephoned Grandma to tell her that they had decided it was best if I did not return. I was effectively expelled.

That meant I would need to go to the local comprehensive school.

Grandma and Aunt Sylvia were convinced this was yet again just prejudice around my home status. I could not help but agree.

I wanted justice, but it was hardly like I could immediately burn the school down. That would prove nothing, and the suspicion would have immediately fallen upon me as the most recently expelled student.

How many students did they expel? I was the first for a few years.

Chapter Eleven

Unlike the boys only school for high achievers, Radnor High was like a loosely controlled war zone.

One of its only redeeming features was that it had girls as well as boys.

Physical bullying was an unofficial sport in the school and one of the few things in my favour was that I arrived as the boy who had allegedly broken the hip and arm of a teacher by pushing them down the stairs.

As I had learnt a few years back from Daz, the only thing bully's respect is strength. Indeed, Daz was a pupil at my new school and one of the most potent bully's the school had to offer. He wasn't that strong, but he had the benefit of a brother at the same school; a boy some three years older than me. He had not had that advantage at primary school.

The school was a melting pot for failure. Even the teachers were effectively the people unable to get work at any decent academic institution.

In the few classes where the teachers were not completely bullied and intimidated by the rogue elements in the class, they had to spend most of their time teaching remedial material. Many of my fellow students were still unable to read or write unless it was a swear word.

Communication was easy as there was only one adjective at the school: an expletive beginning with the letter *f*. I had no idea that a single word could be so versatile:

A further downside: Carl was no longer allowed to be my friend. His dad had decided there was enough of a chance that I might be a wrong 'un to make it wise to bar any contact between Carl and me. Not that it mattered much anyway since we were now at different schools. However, it meant I no longer had access to an insider (his dad) to glean information about how the police handled particular cases.

It was lucky I had enrolled at the town library because I was reasonably sure that acquiring valuable knowledge was important to my future prosperity and that the school was not the place where I would be acquiring it.

I was not entirely correct. The school was a hotbed of criminality and criminal knowledge. From assault to xenophobia, if you wanted to know what the criminals knew, there was a kid at the school whose dad was up to it and happy to share what they knew about how to do it.

In case you are wondering, there is no crime beginning with the letter **z**. Trust me, I would know.

The few months I had spent at the Grammar school had at least shown me what the learning environment should be like, how quick the pace of learning ought to be and what books they were reading. It was all significantly different at Radnor High where the ability to coherently string a sentence together without using a swear word would have been enough to make the alumni list, if they ever had cause to create one, which was doubtful.

I constructed my own curriculum. It included English, Maths, French, Economics, Psychology, Crime and Self-defence. The latter was going to be particularly important if I were to avoid the physical bullying without becoming a member of one of the gangs.

I also made a friend. Cynthia. Terrible name but an amazing girl. She was beautiful, intelligent and when I arrived, the subject of a significant amount of racial torment.

She lived with her mother. Details of her father were sketchy. He was African, her mum had loved him, he wasn't around.

I had never had a friend before. Not a real one. Perhaps it was the early twinkling of puberty. Maybe it was the need to find an excuse to see how much power I could wield, but I was determined to make her life better, to make it clear that she was under my protection and to decimate any bully who so much as called her a name.

I am, as you have probably guessed by now, either a sociopath or a psychopath. That was something neither I nor the authorities knew at that point, but one thing was sure; not even sticks and stones were something I worried about. Not much.

Whatever I am, I believed then as I believe now that the ability not to be ruled by emotions was and is more like a superpower than a disadvantage.

In the first few months, the occasional gang would round on me, but I *always* followed up. I would have bruises and cuts one day and then administer a beating to each person involved, individually, a few days later.

If they were bigger than me, I would bring along a bat.

Bruises and beatings were not something I cared about. I had been hit hard when I was a lot younger by someone much bigger than they were. Dad.

Every gang soon learnt that short of actually killing me, I was going to be someone they should leave alone and once I had established that, I made it clear that also applied to Cynthia.

A few times, the Police were called. Grandma was excellent. I was covered in cuts and bruises from the various beatings, so in the early days I usually looked at least as bad as the complainant.

I got so good at defending myself that I was soon able to tackle small gangs all on my own, even without the aid of my trustee baseball bat.

Another item that had intrigued me at the school for boys was the tackling manoeuvre. Specifically, how a technique without a requirement for strength could conquer an opponent, no matter what his size might be.

I found out that there was a martial art called *Aikido* that was focused on the use of pressure points.

The fighting skills employed by the bullies at my new school were very rudimentary. I managed to get Grandma to sign off on paying for weekly lessons in Aikido and set about mastering the art.

I could soon reduce anyone of any size to a submissive, defeated wreck begging to be released. I stopped short of breaking their arms.

I spent all my spare time learning things, mostly with Cynthia.

One day, she produced a joke shop plastic knife with a blade that retracted into the handle:

"Here Henri, whenever we get something wrong, we can pretend to stab each other."

It amused her so I played along, and we kept that going for many years.

Sometimes we would go walking together, to a picturesque area to the east of Folkestone known as *Little Switzerland*, below the white cliffs.

"It's called Little Switzerland because the steep cliffs and undulating woodlands at the base are very similar to the Swiss countryside." That's what Cynthia told me.

"I guess you have to completely ignore the adjacent wide expanse of sea to believe that." Neither of us laughed. I was just being observant.

I taught Cynthia how to win at Monopoly, she changed the Chance and Community Express cards to liven up the game. Instead of the normal options, the cards had things like; *You have bribed a local official to bypass local planning regulations, you may buy one hotel for the property of your choice even if you do not have the set.*

Or: *Reverse to Mayfair when drunk. Do pass go but pay $200 as a fine for going through the wrong way.*

Or: *You have won second prize in a beauty competition because you are shallow, vain and easily swayed by pretty* *things. Receive $20 from the bank but lose $100 at the party afterwards because you are not very bright.*

We remained close right up until the night of my sixteenth birthday when everything was to change yet again.

Chapter Twelve

Learning how to get extraordinarily rich is, as I now know, a skill.

It is a skill that can be learnt.

More significantly, it is a skill that is self-evidently missing not only from extremely poor people, but also from working class and middle-class people too.

That was unfortunate because in my home network, poor to middle-class people were the only elements of society I ever got to meet.

Ask any of these people how to get rich and you get misleading answers like, *through hard work* or *by becoming an accountant.*

Neither of these approaches will make you billionaire mega-rich.

Super-rich people do not work for other rich people. They have people working for them.

Anyone who is an employee is simply an asset being used by someone else to get richer.

Asking someone who is not at least a self-made millionaire how to get rich is like asking the man who collects the bins how to perform successful brain surgery.

It is possible to become accidentally transiently rich through some incident such as winning a lottery. However, if you follow the average lottery winner for enough years, you will find that the money falls through their hands faster than a child backs out of a bedroom doorway when they accidentally find their parents in flagrante.

That's because the mind of the average lottery winner works like this:

Okay, so I have won £10m on the lottery. I will buy a mansion, a supercar, give half a million to each of my direct relatives and friends, quit my job, buy a modest yacht, travel the world first class, ...and should I tick the publicity box? Why not?

With no income, expensive maintenance bills for what they think are assets (but are actually liabilities) and non-stop begging letters, it does not take long for them to be selling off those items at rock-bottom prices.

As they continue to live a semi-lavish lifestyle with no income, the money completely runs out.

Such people end up back in, or somewhere close to, their original house and back at the same local pub.

They like being back at the local pub, telling stories about when they were rich and how they used to rub shoulders with now forgotten minor celebrities.

Do they miss being rich?

Not at all, they have never been happier than being broke and back home again. That's what they say, but it isn't true.

What are they meant to say?

I am completely incompetent with money. I was totally out of my depth. Everyone could see me coming and I would just get ripped off all the time. I hate being poor again, but I have no idea how to make money.

They still play the lottery, hoping that the numbers may once again come in.

What poor people fail to grasp is the basic difference between assets and liabilities. As a result, money slips through their fingers like water slips through a sieve.

Genuinely rich people know about assets and liabilities.

- Assets are items that earn you money in the here and now.
- Liabilities are items that cost you money to own and maintain.

You may think that something like an expensive house is an asset. It is not. It is a liability because if you live in it or leave it empty, it costs you money to maintain.

If you sell it or rent it out, it can be an asset, as long as the income exceeds all the outgoings, or in the case of selling it, that the price you get exceeds the price you paid when all the additional costs and expenses are taken into consideration.

That is get rich rule number 4:

Gather as many assets together as you can and ensure you have more than enough income from your assets to pay for the liabilities in your life.

Unfortunately, if there was somebody in Folkestone at that time who could have told me about this, I never met him or her. Not at that age.

Chapter Thirteen

By the time my fourteenth birthday arrived I was still poor.

I had come to appreciate Grandma, mad old crone that she was. Grandma was an asset and aside from my intelligence and Cynthia, I had very few of those.

At the age of fourteen, I could finally get some regular paid employment, albeit only at the scandalously low rate of £1 per hour.

A new mini market had recently opened at the top of our street. It was the first shop in town to open from 7am to 11pm and it did so seven days per week.

I was able to start work that very day as a shelf-stacker. I was a hard-worker, and the owner was amenable to me working all the hours I could spare outside of school time. That meant working five hours three evenings per week and a straight eight hours every Saturday and Sunday.

£31 per week and all paid cash in hand at the end of each shift.

I had no illusions that this would make me rich, but for the first time I was able to afford such luxuries as a decent haircut and some new clothes.

Cynthia said I looked like a new person.

Mike was the owner of the store, which he operated with Pete, his boyfriend.

Although Mike was not yet super-rich, he was quite the entrepreneur and had spent most of his time working out how to make money. It was him who taught me about assets and liabilities… although not on paid time.

I would make him a tea or coffee after a shift and pick his brains about how to make money.

Buy low, sell high, pay as little as possible, acquire assets, minimize liabilities.

Mike and Pete liked that I was not in the least bit phased by their relationship. In the mid-eighties, being overtly gay in a small-town was a rare thing and they had occasions where people would enter the store simply to hurl homophobic abuse.

Such prejudicial verbal abuse was nothing the police cared about back then, not unless a person started to smash up the place.

I told Grandma about the abuse. She said it was a pity and that if I really wanted to support them, I should consider getting a boyfriend and not hanging around with Cynthia all the time; "It will be such a disappointment to me if you turn out straight."

Useful, weird input and advice from Grandma as *never.*

With money coming in, my appearance was rapidly transformed from scruffy boy to a slick-suited, brilliant-white shirted, immaculately coiffured young man.

One thing Grandma had in abundance was hairspray and my hair soon became a shrine to eighties fashion. Huge, sculpted quiffs with wet-look strands hanging down.

I might have been able to attract girls but for two

significant problems.

First and foremost, although I had an ability to analyse and project the actions of people, I still had real problems working out what my face should be doing.

I knew how to smile or laugh. I knew how to cry. But I still had significant problems understanding *when* to do these things. For the most part I just kept my expressions as neutral as possible.

My second problem in being able to attract girls; there was only one I was really interested in. *Cynthia.*

Some of the other girls at the school were easy on the eye but seemed to have the mental acuity of a potato.

I determined that there was one particular skill that might help me with both issues: acting.

I joined the local amateur dramatic society. Grandma, with her thespian roots, was overjoyed; perhaps I would turn out to be her kind of grandson after all.

The younger members of the local am-dram met up each Sunday evening.

These meetings provided the opportunity for me to observe the portrayal of an enormous range of different emotions being faked. What I was not able to identify was when this was done badly or well.

My hope was that I would learn how to convert my relationship with Cynthia from friend into boyfriend.

Some of the people the society attracted were particularly prone to over-dramatics. It was like they were the polar opposite to me. They only knew how to be in a constant state of heightened emotion.

This made me grateful for my own condition of complete emotional indifference to almost everything.

It was at the weekly meetups that I met Jake.

Jake was different. In some ways, he was a bit like me. He would stare off at things and not know how to "act" in many situations. It was clear to me that Jake was there for the same reason I was. He wanted to learn how to fit in.

In other ways, Jake was also nothing like me, he liked talking about religion and was not what people would call an academic. He was on an entirely different plane of existence from everyone else.

Jake was a couple of years older than me. I recall sitting in the town centre one winter evening, aged fifteen and seeing Jake cycling precariously at low speed through the pedestrian precinct. He didn't notice me. I was eating some takeaway fish and chips. I don't think he would have noticed if spaceships had been flying around.

He was though, noticed by a couple of police constables that were doing the rounds. They stopped Jake and the conversation was an education for me. It went like this.

"Oy, you on the bike. STOP." These words came from the older of the two officers. It looked like one was a training officer and the other was a trainee.

"You've got no lights on your bike. It's illegal to ride during the hours of darkness without lights. We can arrest you for that." The officer looked at his rookie smugly, he was going to show his inexperienced colleague how to make an arrest, so he thought.

"In addition…" continued the older officer," you are riding around in a pedestrian area. That is also illegal. You need to get off your bike *now*." The lead officer by this time was firmly gripping the middle front of the bike handlebars.

I was transfixed, I had never seen an arrest before, and it was like someone had laid this on as entertainment during my outdoor evening meal.

Jake got unsteadily off his pedal bike. His first words to the policemen were "I'm terribly sorry officers, it's just I've had so much to drink this afternoon."

In the history of suppressed happy grins, I have never seen a police officer with a larger one trying not to appear. Drunk, no lights, riding where riding is forbidden and confessing to it all. They could throw the book at him.

The officer was getting the cuffs out as the conversation was continuing, at least from Jake. How unhappy he was, troubles with his parents, …

By this time, the cuffs were on and behind his back. The officers were on foot and would need to arrange for a car to collect him.

…his theories about God.

As Jake mentioned God, I could see the lead officer pause and narrow his eyes. It was like the G-word was some kind of warning trigger.

"Oh, I am so sorry." Continued Jake. "I am so stoned. I guess marijuana and alcohol don't mix."

Could he dig himself any deeper? Yes.

"You don't know where I could get some more drugs do you?"

There was a dawning realization on the face of the lead officer that he had clearly found someone who was what the police of the time referred to as a *nut-job*.

Within thirty seconds, the cuffs were off, and Jake was back on his bike, in the pedestrian area. The police officers were wishing him well and he was being encouraged to cycle on without lights.

"It's probably better if you arrest me" was all I remember hearing as the officers wandered off down the precinct pursued by Jake at a low, wobbly speed on his bike.

"Go away" one of them eventually shouted and I saw Jake wobble off in a different direction.

Amazing. He had just got out of an arrest by being insanely stupid. It was possibly one of the cleverest, stupid things I have seen to this day.

Chapter Fourteen

Sometime in 1985, the school acquired some computers and installed a small network. A small fleet of eight RM Nimbus computers were assembled and connected together in a classroom that had been renamed *the computer room*.

Finally, I would be able to really work on acquiring some programming skills.

One of the mathematics teachers, Mr Granger, a greasy guy with thick spectacles and no wife, was put in charge of the room. His two-favourite past-times appeared to be reading computer manuals and picking his nose.

With only eight computers and over a thousand students, I had thought that getting use of the computers might be a challenge. Fortunately, the generally low academic standard, coupled with the regular anti-aesthetic presence of Mr Granger meant that other than class times, the computers were rarely in use.

Cynthia, like me, was also interested in computers. In her words, computers just followed instructions and had no prejudice.

As it turned out, Cynthia had quite the brain for maths and was practically a savant at picking up programming skills. She was far better at it than I was. She was much better at it than Mr Granger was.

In return for all the skills I helped Cynthia with,

she, in turn helped progress my own programming ability. We helped each other because ultimately that helped each of us.

One particular day, Cynthia told me she had some really amazing new computer skills to teach me. She was working on a multi-user program and needed to borrow my username and password to set-up the lesson.

I willingly obliged.

A few hours later, I was called out of class and summoned to Mr Granger in the computer room.

As I entered the room, there was an unruly class making their own entertainment. Why weren't they working on some basic computer thing?

I looked around the room. On each screen there was a very rudimentary graphic of a smiling face and underneath were the words *"Have a cookie."*

"Henri," said Mr Granger sternly. "Our network seems to have acquired a virus and according to the log on the file server, it belongs to you. So, I suggest you remove it right now and then I can remove your computer room privileges for the next month."

I raised my eyebrows. I had no idea how to get rid of the virus. I had a feeling I knew who did, but I was not about to give her away.

There was a long and awkward pause. Then, finally I said; "I would love to help sir. Erm…"

There was a second awkward pause.

Mr Granger's eyes narrowed, and you could see the realization cross his face that this feat was beyond my own abilities and there was only one person up to the task.

His lips seethed just one word:" Cynthia." He sent another student to get her.

According to Cynthia, the lesson I needed to learn from this was to never trust anyone with my username and password. In return, I told her the lesson she should learn is to never be the only plausible suspect in a crime.

We were both banned from the computer room for a month.

Chapter Fifteen

Success!

By the time I reached my fifteenth birthday, Cynthia and I were a proper item.

Her mother did not approve.

It was not me Cynthia's mother objected to. As far as her mother was concerned, Cynthia should not be dating anyone until she was at least thirty. Perhaps this was because Cynthia's mother, Glenda, had got pregnant so young. Maybe Glenda was joking. I was unsure. Humour was yet another emotion lost on me.

One more thing that confused me was that Cynthia's mother would regularly sunbathe topless in her back garden. Apparently, it was okay for me to see *Glenda's* boobs but not those of her daughter. How was that okay?

I would sleep over occasionally but always in the spare room and her mother would sleep with her own door open to ensure there were no illegal night manoeuvres.

The night before my sixteenth birthday, I slept over at Cynthia's house.

I have always been a light sleeper, able to rapidly come back into consciousness if I hear anything. At about 3 am I heard something. Someone was coming into my bedroom.

Seconds later, there was a hand on my shoulder. I

looked up suddenly awake. It was Cynthia's mother.

Hell's teeth. Perhaps this explained why she was always so relaxed about me seeing her topless.

She spoke softly and quietly.

"Erm. I have the police on the phone. It's about your grandmother. Someone broke into her house. She heard them and screamed. One of the neighbours called the police. The police are there now, but she is quite worried and asked if you might come home."

Within two minutes I slipped my day clothes on and headed out of the door.

It was a one mile walk between Cynthia's house and my own. I set off down her long street until I reached the main road.

As I turned for home, I was surprised to hear my name shouted from across the street; "Henri!"

I looked across the street. On the main road, the bleak sodium-orange glow of streetlights marginally offset the darkness. *It looked like Jake.* It *was* Jake.

I continued home as Jake hurried up alongside me.

He told me why he was out so early in the morning. His parents had thrown him out.

Jake was an open book. He told me that his parents had taken him to see a psychiatrist after he hit them. The Psychiatrist had diagnosed Jake as a paranoid schizophrenic.

Did I think he was paranoid? Not at all.

I was sympathetic but told him the reason I was out and why I needed to get back. He said he would walk with me.

I did not want him to, but I knew that trying to push him away would be pointless, so I let him walk with me.

We passed a second-hand shop. It was a run-down part of town and to add to the ambience – the store had left assorted items of worthless junk on the pavement in front. Presumably, this was in the hope that someone might remove or redistribute some of the items overnight.

This included a solitary broken wooden dining chair with one leg hanging off. As we passed the store, Jake broke off the chair leg and then began falling back and running up on me with it in a set of simulated attack runs.

Great. This was not the overhead I needed right now. Given Jake's mental state, I thought he might just whack me over the head without realizing what he was doing.

I put my hand in my pocket. *What was that?* In my pocket I felt a hard, springy object. I had Cynthia's joke shop knife that we used as our study incentive. I had an idea. Distract Jake with the novelty knife.

"Here, why don't have this pretend knife. It's even better."

With little persuasion, Jake put the chair leg down and eagerly studied the joke shop knife.

He soon began running up and down around me, plunging the mock blade into my chest and back.

That was okay. I just hoped he didn't have a real knife that he might substitute on one of his attack runs.

Once we reached the top of my street, I was determined to lose Jake before I got home. I didn't want him to know exactly where I lived.

"This is me. I had better leave you here and get back."

I had to engage him in a further fifteen minutes of conversation before he finally got the message that I was going down my street alone. I watched as he wandered off into the distance.

Confident he was gone I made my way down my street to Grandma's front door. It was now about thirty minutes since the police had called.

There were no signs of forced entry. The burglar or burglars had slipped the lock. My key still worked.

Two police officers, a man and a woman sat with Grandma in the kitchen. They told me that, as far as they could tell. nothing had been taken, the burglar or burglars had left the building when Grandma had screamed.

They told me I should check my room and see if the thieves had stolen anything.

My first thought was for the only item of alleged value in my room. *Please. Let them have taken my piano accordion.*

The police officers were enjoying one of Grandma's cups of tea. *Good luck with that*, I thought. Undoubtedly, she had used one of the teacups she had washed herself. Such cups would invariably have dried, powdered chicken soup residue at the bottom, but you usually only found that out during the final third of the drink.

I made my way up to my room, marvelling at how

disappointed any burglar must have been at the contents of Grandma's house.

My room was still spick and span. Sadly, the piano accordion was still in its box in the cupboard.

The only thing unusual and out of place, was a huge pair of novelty size underpants in the middle of the floor.

They were not mine.

To be honest, they did not look to be of a size suitable for any human. I would have guessed they might fit Jabba the Hut.

I was bigger now, just a bit shorter than the average adult, but I was still extremely thin. There was no sane explanation for the presence of such sizable underpants.

In my room, there was a boarded-up fireplace with an old stone mantel piece that I used to store my stationery. I picked up a biro from the mantel piece. As I had seen on episodes of *Quincy* (a police forensics TV programme), I put the pen inside the pants and lifted them off the ground. It was apparent from the grey colour and the subtle brown track inside, that these underpants were not new, and not even appropriately washed.

What the hell was going on?

My mind whizzed through everything I had ever seen or learnt about burglaries.

At the drama classes, one boy had recently told his friends an urban legend about *the toothbrush burglars*. You may have heard of this:

A newly married couple head off on honeymoon. When they

return home, the couple discover that a burglary has taken place. The thieves have taken everything, aside from two toothbrushes and a partially used disposable camera they had. Furniture, carpets, cooker; everything was stolen.

They set about replacing everything else apart from the camera and toothbrushes.

Months later they finally use the last shots in the disposable camera and then send the film off to be developed.

When the photos arrive, they are shocked to discover a rogue photo in the middle of the pictures. It has two men's bottoms in view with the handle of a toothbrush protruding out of each.

Maybe that's what this is. Like the toothbrush burglars. Maybe these are the *underpants burglars*, this is their calling card and there is some sting in the tail… no pun intended.

With this thought in mind, I walked down the stairs brandishing the underpants on the end of my pen to preserve any potential forensic evidence, naïve as I was.

As I got to the top of the stairs down to the kitchen, I put the underpants behind my back.

I could see the police officers were now somewhere in the last third of their drinks. The male officer was squinting and looking into the cup trying to discern where the chicken taste was coming from.

He was happy for the excuse to put the drink down; "Anything missing?" He asked.

"There was nothing missing," I said, "But I did find these, and they are definitely not mine." I then produced the novelty-size underpants-evidence from behind my back.

The police officers were really intrigued. They took the pen from me and started to look around and inside the evidence. They too appeared to recoil as they discovered the inner track mark.

From the chair in the corner, Grandma was squinting, straining her poor eyesight to see what we were looking at. After about ten seconds, she seemed to recognize the image, stopped squinting and spoke.

"Oh those. I found them at a charity store, and I thought they might fit you. I know you're growing."

For the record, I never wore used underpants. It was not exactly something I could say to the police at that time.

The police officers fell into fits of laughter.

I sunk my head and retired to bed. At least tomorrow was a Friday, my sixteenth birthday and as it was early September, the new school term did not begin until Monday, so I could have a lay-in.

The next morning, I was up and ready to go by 10am. I was going to meet Cynthia and tell her what had happened.

I opened my front door, now almost recovered from my previous night and ready to head to Cynthia's house. The terraced house emerged straight onto the street.

As I opened the door, Jake walked past as casually as if he was a neighbour happening by; *"Morning,"* he said and stared at me for just the wrong amount of time for it to be comfortable.

Chapter Sixteen

This was the very last night of my childhood.

The police had thought the break-in was just some random, ill-targeted burglary attempt but I was going to find out that was not the case.

Aside from Jake clearly identifying where I lived, the day passed as normal. Terrible gift from Grandma, a book on *How to Play the Piano Accordion* now I was big enough to lift it.

Cynthia had bought me a sweater. I wore it to her place.

Aunt Sylvia had given me the usual book voucher.

Through hard work and perseverance, not to mention higher weekly wages as I grew older, I had managed to put aside nearly £1,800 in savings at the bank.

I had one more year to complete at Radnor High before I could change schools.

When I went to bed that night, I had no idea about what was going to happen next.

I awoke suddenly sometime early in the morning. I could not tell you exactly what time because the last thing I felt was an arm around my neck pulling tightly. My eyes bulged and seconds later I was out cold. There was no time to put any of my Aikido skills into action.

I came around briefly, it was still dark, my upper

arm was sore, and I could smell something pungent.

For a fraction of a second before I passed out again, I saw a blurry figure with a scarf covering his face mouth and nose. There was something unmistakable about those eyes and had I heard a foot dragging?

I was sure of who it was.

Canning.

When I came too again it was dawn.

It took me a while to get my bearings.

I felt groggy, I was shivering and felt sick, really sick. The nausea felt overwhelming. It took me time to gather myself enough to sit up and put my legs over the side of the bed.

I had engaged in some underage drinking on a few occasions, and this felt considerably worse than any hangover I had experienced.

I threw up a little on the floor. As I did so, I noticed my baseball bat was in a different position from its usual resting place.

As my mind began to clear, I realized the top end of the baseball bat was covered in blood.

I looked myself over. No blood.

Where else could the blood have come from?

Grandma.

I struggled to my feet. I opened the door to my room. I staggered up the staircase to her room, grabbing the handrail for support.

Grandma was in her bed. There was a significant amount of blood. Her head looked like it had been on the receiving end of my baseball bat.

She was clearly dead.

Very dead.

I ran through events in my mind; *Canning's face, the attempted burglary the previous night must have been him too. He must have abandoned it when he realized I was not at home. But why?*

I thought about this more; *Why did he knock me out and not kill me?*

Of course. He wanted to ruin me. He wanted me to suffer the way he had by ruining his life. He wanted my fingerprints on whatever weapon he used to kill Grandma.

Should I call the police?

On the one hand, there was me, a social misfit with a history of being in trouble with the police and my fingerprints on the murder weapon.

On the other, Mr Canning, who I was certain would have prepared an alibi.

I had to think quickly. *How was I going to be able to deal with this?*

I took a moment to say thank you to Grandma and to apologize to her for not being more grateful. Despite my muted emotions, this was an intense moment, and I felt my eyes well up slightly. It was the closest I have ever come to shedding real tears.

Was Mr Canning going to call the police? I doubted it, too incriminating, but I would not be able to hide this for too long or he certainly would find a way of bringing them to my door.

Should I withdraw my savings and go on the run? That would make me look entirely guilty. How much did I have at the house? How much did Grandma have?

All the money in the house totalled a paltry £24.98.

I sat hunched over in a chair in the corner of Grandma's room. By now I had a severe headache. I surmised this was the after effect of whatever drug Canning had used to knock me out.

I sat there for a good ninety minutes, waiting for the head pain to clear. By the end of the ninety minutes, I had a plan.

It was time for Henri Jones to die.

Chapter Seventeen

It would be too suspicious for Henri Jones to leave a suicide note and then never have his body discovered, especially after the brutal murder of his grandmother.

There would be no way to contact Cynthia or let her know what happened or what I was doing. I could not afford to let anyone in on my plans.

The first thing I needed was a second corpse.

It needed to be about my size and age. Preferably it should be someone who almost nobody cared about.

Darren Pearson was the clear option.

Daz was a similar height and build to me and he lived just six houses away. Another set of pluses were that nobody liked him, *and* he had a worse reputation with the local law enforcement than I did.

It might look suspicious that he disappeared at the same time I died, but I would find a way to divert attention.

It was not a perfect plan, but time was pressing, and it was the only viable option I could think up this swiftly. Even so, I would need a degree of luck to pull this off.

The first thing I needed to do was to get Daz on his own and preferably into my house.

I checked the time; it was just gone eight in the morning.

I had to wait patiently for Daz to appear. As I monitored the street from behind the net curtains in the upstairs lounge, I began to write into a new notebook. I was constructing a diary with entries for the past three months. It included real events, thoughts about Cynthia but also a fictional narrative; repeated concerns about escalating threats I alleged to be receiving from Daz.

He had threatened to kill me. He had threatened to kill Grandma. I was worried for my life.

I embellished the entry for today. *Had the burglary last night been Daz? Had he left because I was not there? I dare not share my suspicions with the police because then Daz would definitely be after me.*

After two hours Daz finally emerged, he was on his own, wheeling out his BMX.

I went into the street and encouraged him over, he rested his bike on the railings of his house. "What do *you* want?"

"I've found a way of making a lot of money, but I need help right now and I'm willing to cut you in."

He looked suspicious. I rustled the two £10 notes I had in his direction. He grabbed and pocketed them. I told him there were more where they came from. He was in.

I led him into the house through the back garden.

"Upstairs" I said. I took him to the top of the house. I had moved the bloodied bat into Grandma's room.

"Where are we going?" he asked.

"You'll see."

I walked into the bedroom first and lifted the bat. As he entered the room he looked around and immediately saw Grandma's corpse.

"What the…"

These were the last words of Darren Pearson. I wondered how many people shared those same last words as the bat hit the side of his head.

I hit him quite a few more times to be sure he was definitely never going to be getting up again. I didn't feel good about this. The truth be told, I didn't feel much about anything.

Daz had something I needed. A spare body of roughly the right size and shape. It might not have been spare from Darren's perspective, but I was not thinking from his viewpoint, I was thinking from my own.

What useful contribution was Daz ever going to make to society? If you really think about it, it was a kindness. Not a kindness to Darren, but a kindness to humanity.

I went to my room and packed a small rucksack, being careful to leave behind my passport. I had one from going on school daytrips to France, but if I took it, then it would be clear the corpse upstairs was not me.

I knew that dental records were a thing. I had never had any dental work, but what about Daz? I checked his mouth. I could not see any. His teeth were straighter than mine, so I added an extra whack of the baseball bat to that area. It would have to do.

I checked his pockets. He only had the £20 I lured

him in with and a door key. Shame.

I took the money back and put it in my pocket. I pulled the clothes off his corpse. I dressed Daz into a set of my own clothes. I wrapped his clothes and his key into a plastic bag and put them in my rucksack.

I placed my newly written diary on the lower floor where my bedroom was located.

Grandma was still using paraffin heaters in the winter. Fortunately, we had quite a bit of paraffin in the house. I spread the flammable accelerant around the upper staircase and bodies.

By the time I struck the match, it was late morning.

I was careful to leave through the back door, leaving it unlocked. Leaving it unlocked in the daytime was nothing unusual.

As I left the garden through the back gate, the cats started to stream out of the cat flap, already sensing the need to seek alternative accommodation.

I took the most expedient set of back alleys and secondary routes out of Folkestone towards the bypass where there were usually at six or more continental trucks parked up.

About half an hour later, I could see a small pillar of black smoke rising from Grandma's house about a mile back in the distance

I had £24.98, the clothes I was in, a backpack with a change of clothes, one spare t-shirt and nothing else. Canning's actions had wiped me out.

I needed to find a way of starting my life over. And I needed to get out of town, fast.

ACT 2: Rebirth

Chapter Eighteen

I know what you might be thinking, but honestly, Darren was the first person that I have ever killed. Unless you include my twin brother.

What? You thought I killed my own father? I was only eight at the time dad fell on those train tracks. I was at home in bed when it happened. Shame on you.

You think I killed Daz's friend too?

What kind of person ties a plastic bag with string around the head of an eight-year-old boy? Not me.

Sure, I had followed him for a while after beating up Daz, but then I had gone home.

What reason would I have to lie to you?

Even the death of my brother was not necessarily my fault. I was too young to remember what happened. Clearly it must, at worst, have been an accident.

It is true that I framed Mr Canning and cut his brakes but as it turned out, he definitely deserved it.

All that said, there are certain lines that are better to never cross and murder might be one of them. I say *might be* because, well, you will see. What I can tell you now is that my fortune, or curse, is that innate emotional detachment I have. Perhaps this was something with which I was born? Or maybe this was a result of my early childhood experiences? Maybe it was both. I couldn't tell you.

Murdering someone had proven to be far easier than I thought. I didn't feel bad about it. I didn't feel good about it. It had just been a necessary action to get me out of an immediate problem. It certainly seemed to me like a pragmatic and viable choice for solving future disputes.

Now I had a new set of problems. I was on the run for my life, or at least for my freedom, nearly penniless and everything I had as Henri Jones was lost, burnt to a crisp. Even my hard-earned savings were beyond reach.

Everything was gone. My clothes, my money, my… It was then I realized how little I had so far achieved. What else did I have to show from my first sixteen years of life? A piano accordion? A friendship with Cynthia. I would miss that. Cynthia, I mean. I would not miss the piano accordion.

My adrenaline had been pumping hard for hours. The headache had finally gone, I was hungry, but I dare not enter any shop for fear of being seen and retrospectively recognized at a time when Henri

Jones was supposed to be dead.

A double homicide with a missing murderer was bound to grab headline news. I needed to get as far away as possible.

My expectation was that the manhunt would focus on Daz, but almost certainly the papers would have pictures of Grandma and I too as the bludgeoned and burnt victims of his alleged crime.

Given that I was bilingual, on the run and living close to a channel port, there was a clear and optimal direction of travel for me. France.

It was part of the reason I had left my British passport behind. If I had taken it with, eventually, the police might figure out that it was missing and suspect the corpse was not mine and that I had headed out of the country. But if I could get across the border undetected, the language barrier and general disinterest between France and the UK should make my getaway easier.

I was sure I could still speak French like a native.

French, or at least native French, has a vastly different rhythm from English. It has evenly spaced syllables. That is the reason that native French people trying to speak English sound so obviously French. They speak each British syllable like it is the tick-tock of a clock. *When-I-was-young-er-I-liv-ed-in-Par-is.*

I had the same problem when I first arrived in the UK.

English, native English does not have that rhythm. It has stress points in certain words and syllables are either rushed or relaxed between the stress points. It had taken me a while to perfect sounding native English, but it would be no issue for me to sound native French because that was my true origin.

I could not wait until dark, I had to get out of the country as soon as possible.

Could I bribe one of the truckers passing through to sneak me across the border without a passport? That would be too risky. Any French trucker would be unlikely to do this for £24.98 and anyway, they might deduce who I was later, based on the news headlines and my point of departure.

I finally arrived at the Folkestone bypass and at the Dover-bound lay-by where seven trucks were parked, mostly with drivers taking a nap or a break prior to heading for the cross-channel ferry.

The bypass was a busy road with vehicles zipping through in both directions at sixty miles per hour. The lay-by was a small and uneven track of land, barely the width of a truck and had the pungent stench of urine in the air. The noise, smell and speed of passing traffic meant that it was unlikely I would be noticed if I stayed on the offside of the trucks.

I tried to nonchalantly wander down the row looking at the foreign registered trucks for potential areas to hide unnoticed.

The rear of each truck had a mechanism which would require someone to close it from the outside. That would be no use.

I bent down to inspect the underside. There were areas where I might be able to hold on, but it all looked too precarious. Besides, border control would certainly notice anyone that stupidly exposed.

One of the trucks had a Parisienne haulage sign.

I revisited my options. I could not risk remaining in Folkestone. I could not quickly or easily walk the eight miles to Dover and even if I did, I would just have the same problem when I got there; no passport and no transport to hide on.

Four of the trucks had canvas sides, but without a knife, I would not be able to cut my way in and besides, a truck with cut canvas was sure to attract attention at the border.

From my experience of day trips to France, customs were not expecting smugglers to take anything out of the UK. The border checks focused on inbound vehicles, looking for low-priced cigarettes, wine or for drugs.

I noticed on the roof of the driver's cab of the Parisienne truck, there was a spoiler with what looked like a recess behind it. There was also a vertical set of rungs, a ladder, built-in to the front edge of the trailer. I climbed up between the cab and the trailer and jumped across, landing as quietly as I could on the roof of the cab. I swung myself and my rucksack into the space under the roof spoiler, again being careful to make as little sound as possible.

There was little room between the three-sided spoiler and the roof of the truck, but I was still very slim, so I squeezed as far forward as possible. Hopefully, that would keep me hidden, if nobody shone a light into the recess.

It was early September and not too cold. The

spoiler was like a short three-sided hut. I anticipated this should protect me from the wind chill.

It was an hour before I heard the engine start and I could feel the truck pulling away. When the truck began to climb the hill out of Folkestone, I discovered a new dilemma as I started to slide backwards. I jammed my hands and legs to wedge myself between the ceiling of the three-sided spoiler and the roof of the cab, with my rucksack hooked over one arm and sliding out from under the spoiler. Dover Hill must be one of the longest and steepest roadways in Britain. The truck crawled up it very slowly. It was probably only 3 minutes but by the time it reached the top my muscles were stinging with pain.

For the rest of the journey, I found myself needing to alternate between resting my muscles and suddenly pressing against the spoiler shell for dear life.

Twenty minutes later I could feel the truck idle and crawl intermittently. Hopefully, he was in the queue for the ferry. I lay as still and silently as possible. I heard the driver tell the border check he was returning empty. *Did he have any passengers?* No, he did not.

They checked his passport and waved him through.

Thirty minutes later the truck was climbing the ramp into the ferry. By now my rucksack was across my front.

Once the truck was parked inside the ferry, the

engine was turned off. I heard the driver leave the truck and lock the door. I dare not move from my position until we were safely through and into France. I lay there for the next two hours and could feel the gentle roll and buffing of the English Channel as whatever ferry we were on made the crossing.

On the other side, Calais I think, it took a further thirty minutes for the truck to disembark and clear the French border control.

There were the same questions, now in French.

I had made it to France, but I still needed to remain unnoticed.

There was no way I was going to survive a lengthy road journey pressed into the roof spoiler. Once we left the port boundary, I banged my fist three times on the roof. The truck slowed slightly. It was crawling around the exit road for Calais.

I banged again.

This time the trucks air brakes began to intermittently hiss as the truck pulled over on to the side of the road. Once it was below about ten miles per hour, I made my move. I pulled myself out from underneath the spoiler, jumped across to the trailer, climbed down the steel ladder on the front of the trailer and waited on the bottom rung for the truck to come to a dead stop.

Timing was important.

I waited until I heard the driver's door open, so that I could be reasonably sure the driver would not be looking at the wing mirror on the passenger door.

I dropped as quietly as possible on the passenger side of the truck and around to the front, as the driver made his way backwards so he could look at the roof of his cab.

I stopped about twenty feet in front of the truck before turning around, dropping my rucksack on the ground, and holding my thumb out for a lift.

When the driver turned around, he jumped a little. *Where had I come from. Had I been on the roof?*

I picked up my rucksack and joined him and we both tried to peer at the roof-space from the ground together.

"But no. Not me," I said in my most authentic and native sounding French. "Maybe it was an immigrant? I think I did see somebody jump off a few hundred metres back. Are you going to Paris by any chance?"

The driver was a short, stocky, untidy middle-aged man. He looked like he hadn't shaved for a few weeks. I noticed his eyes were pointing in slightly different directions which made it difficult to know which one to look at.

"That must be the wisest immigrant ever. They usually want to go the other way." He pointed back towards the UK. "For the shitty English food, I guess."

"Paris?" I asked.

He grunted. I couldn't tell if it was acceptance or rejection.

"Are you not afraid of travelling with a truck driver?" he asked. "You know we are all crazy, unwashed murderers who spend our weekends blocking roads."

I told him I was not nervous.

"Okay then, jump in."

Yes!

As I climbed up the passenger side into the cabin, I could smell the wreak of tobacco and unventilated farts, but it was warmer in the cab than on the roof, I was tired and thirsty, and I did not care.

As the truck pulled away, I wanted nothing more than to sleep, but the driver seemed insistent on talking. This was clearly going to be my payment for the ride.

He was fed up with being stereotyped as a trucker.

"We are not all murderers you know. Do I look like a murderer?"

No, he did not.

What does a murderer look like anyway? I had told him that I thought they came in all shapes and sizes.

"Being a truck driver is like one of those Catch-23 situations."

Catch-23? I had only heard of Catch-22. Perhaps the book had a sequel?

"When you have no qualifications, truck driving is the best job you can hope for. But shaving and keeping clean on the road is hard, so then you begin to look like the stereotype. Then all the driving and isolation, it sends you a bit cuckoo. Eventually, you just hang around with other drivers and why not use that time for peaceful protest? Then finally you are so close to the truck-driving stereotype, nobody wants to hire you for anything else." He paused.

"But I have never murdered anyone. What about you?"

He looked at me.

"Hardly ever," I said. "Honestly in the big scheme of things, it's such a small fraction of my time I have spent murdering people…" The truck driver laughed.

"No. I meant what is your story? How is such a young man out travelling alone from Calais to Paris?"

I concocted a story. *A girlfriend in Calais, no money for the train and a working mother in Paris.*

"Renaud," he said. At first, I thought he was saying *Renault*, like the French car and truck manufacturer. Then he clarified; "My name is Renaud, with a *d*."

As my mind was working through the potential challenges a truck driver called Renaud might have given that he was driving a Volvo. I suddenly realized I did not yet have a name I could use.

"Eugène" I finally said. It was the name of another kid from my nursery school in Paris.

Renaud pulled a canteen from the side pocket in his door. He precariously unscrewed the lid using the same hand he was using to steer the truck, then swigged from the bottle. I was so thirsty. My eyes were staring lustily at the bottle. Renaud glanced sideways and noticed.

He thrust the bottle sideways at me. "You want some?"

Yes, I did. I took a huge swig from the bottle and involuntarily sprayed it all back around the cab. What the heck was that? The smell was faintly familiar from my infancy. It certainly wasn't water.

"A nice Merlot," said Renaud, seemingly unphased by the red wine dripping around the cab. Given the state of the cab that was not necessarily a surprise. "It is the fuel of the French working man."

I asked Renaud if he had any water. He moved his head from side-to-side, shrugged and then added "No" just in case I had not got the message. "But we will stop in a couple of hours for something to eat. They will have water in the toilet."

Then he seemed to have some kind of thought and started excitedly pointing at the small bunk behind the seats.

"I think I might have one bottle of German white wine back there. That is pretty much like water. But be careful not to drink from the yellow bottles. They are not water."

Renaud seemed to reflect for a moment, "Although the yellow bottles may taste better than the German wine… And come to think of it, they probably have a higher alcohol content too."

As we drove towards Paris, I looked out across the countryside. Unlike my former home in the UK, the landscapes in France rolled on for miles without another road or building in sight. Back in Kent, it was never possible to go more than a few hundred meters without stumbling on to a country road or structure of one type or another.

Renaud told me a little about his life. I asked him how old he was. He looked middle-aged to me.

"Twenty-three." He said with a completely straight face.

"No way." He must have had a hard life.

He was joking, he was forty-three. He still must have had a hard life because I would have put his age closer to sixty.

I told him about my aspirations to become rich. The three get rich rules I had learnt so far; *research your market, create a monopoly, acquire assets*. Of course, there were four rules I had acquired by then, but telling Renaud that *taking at every opportunity* was a good approach seemed contrary to my current situation. I needed Renaud to give me as much help as possible.

I told Renaud about my studies of how self-made rich people got rich. Pierre Deveraux for example, the wealthy Parisienne who had made his fortune in pharmaceuticals.

Renaud pulled a face of slight disgust. "He is a rogue you know, a dangerous criminal. He made his money through crime. It is well known in Paris, but he has the police in his pocket."

I did not know that. It certainly was not in his autobiography. Although, his autobiography did talk at length in the beginning about his time in the French resistance during the Second World War.

A few hours into the journey, Renaud told me we were going to stop for something to eat. I explained that I only had English money on me.

"It was from a day-trip to Dover with my girlfriend and I forgot to change it back," I had said.

Renaud kindly agreed to change £10 of my English money into one hundred Francs. He was going backwards and forwards to the UK, so it was no problem.

By the time we stopped it was seven o'clock at night. The daylight was beginning to fade.

I had not eaten for a day.

"You are in for a treat. One of the perks for *les routiers…*" (the truckers) "is the *carte routiers.*" (The truckers' menu).

He was not wrong. The set menu consisted of three-courses, *charcuterie,* or cold meats to start, a beef steak with French fries for the main course and a thick, fresh yogurt for dessert, a bargain at a mere ten francs, with a further five francs for the large carafe of red wine.

Renaud's fellow truckers were a sociable lot. Some of them knew each other, most of them did not, but they all sat together and shared their stories of the road as they quaffed copious amounts of wine.

After downing a considerable amount of water, I had some wine too. Drinking from an early age is normal in France. It would not matter if I had been ten years old, as long as I had an adult with me. Besides, I had told Renaud I was eighteen, but just young-looking for my age.

By the time the meal was done, the entire group of truckers were beyond tipsy. I thought this meant we would each be sleeping in our trucks until morning, but to my surprise at about nine o'clock they all got up and made their way back to their respective juggernauts to continue their journeys.

Nine heavy goods vehicles weaved gently on to the quiet backroad where the café was situated. The trucks departed into the two different directions, either towards Paris or Calais.

Despite my fear of Renaud crashing the truck in his drunken state, the combination of exhaustion and wine finally got to me, and I slept for most of the remaining journey.

It was four more hours until we hit central Paris.

Renaud kindly dropped me off on the Boulevard Clichy. He scribbled his home phone number on a piece of paper; "If you ever get rich or need a truck driver, feel free to leave me a message."

He asked if I was sure I wanted to be dropped off there. I told him I lived nearby on the Avenue Rachel, which was almost true. That was where dad's apartment had been.

Chapter Nineteen

I had little idea about what to do next. It was nearly eight years since I was last in Paris, and I was only a young child back then. Would my remaining eighty-five francs be enough to get a room for the night? Could I save the money and sleep outdoors somewhere?

I knew the area around my childhood apartment reasonably well. It was rough and full of crime late at night. On the few occasions I had been out at that time, I had been largely ignored. Nobody was interested in a young boy, but now I was a young man.

As Renaud's truck pulled away into the distance, I decided to head down to a small park in the Place Adolphe Max. There might be a bench I could sleep on until morning.

The main street was still busy with late night revellers, it was the tail end of a Saturday night. As I headed down the side street, I was not immediately aware that someone had followed me. The first thing I knew was when he shouted, "Hey."

I turned around. It was a man in his early twenties.

"That's a nice rucksack you have there." he said in French.

My shoulders sagged. He was talking about the rucksack on my back. The one containing the incriminating clothes I had peeled from the corpse of

Darren Pearson.

"Do you have any money?"

I turned away and began to walk off.

He ran up to and ahead of me.

"Hey, don't walk away from me little man. That is just rude."

I closed my eyes and breathed gently in and out to gain my focus. I had both straps of my rucksack in the right place over each shoulder. In my mind I ran back through my Aikido training; *The fight is a river. I must blend with the river.*

"Look, I don't want any trouble. I don't have anything of interest. This is everything I have in the world." I pointed my thumb at the rucksack on my back.

Unfortunately, from the smile that broadened across the man's face, my words seemed to mark me out as an even more attractive target. The man was now stood about two feet in front of me. He produced a large knife.

"Why don't you let me work out what I can leave you with?"

Folkestone had been full of unsophisticated fighters, but I could see from the way this man held the knife he knew what he was doing. He held his wrist down and the knife up. I knew that someone who does not know how to hold a knife leaves his wrist exposed and striking the wrist makes them drop the weapon. His wrist was not exposed.

If it came to a fight, the first move would be decisive. If I tried to fight him, it was almost certain one of us would end up bleeding in the street.

As a spoiler alert, I should tell you that I was the one who would shortly be bleeding in the street.

"Please," I said. The word surprised me. I don't think I had ever said the word please before.

"Come on," he said and gestured with his other hand for me to hand over everything I had.

I closed my eyes again to focus and visualize what I needed to do. *Evade, off-balance, throw. You must not step in on your opponent or they will gain the advantage.*

There was a moment when he saw the defiance in my eyes and the blade flashed forwards. *Tenkan*, I turned to evade the attack and grabbed his wrist, using his own energy in a dynamic reversal. *Kotegaeishi*, he was in a wrist lock.

In Folkestone this would have worked, but to my surprise he reversed the motion and the knife slipped past my side. I felt a searing pain. I could see my jacket and side was cut.

He was stood back from me now and dancing from foot to foot; "Come on then little man, you want to fight for it."

I really did not. I stood my ground and watched his movements. I needed to raise my game. As he came forwards, *munetsuki* (mid-strike), I hit him as hard as I could in the solar plexus. I had pictured his solar plexus being twelve inches behind where it really was to ensure the punch had enough force. I hit him with such force it hurt my hand. As he folded over, I added a neck punch, grabbed the wrist that held the knife, kicked my leg into the air around his shoulder and flipped him to the ground using my entire body weight for the momentum.

He lay on the ground with his arm in the air. I had him pinned, but I needed to press the advantage because I was not sure I would be able to catch him out again. This was a battle for survival, and he probably knew how to come back from this. He had already come back from my attempt at a wrist lock.

I performed a knee drop on to the back of his neck. There was a crunch as I landed. I had never done this with my full force before. I thought that crunch may well have been his neck breaking.

I kicked his knife away into the gutter and looked around. There was nobody else in sight.

I looked at him. He was face down and motionless. I rolled him over and I could see his eyes were wide open and his pupils were fixed and dilated.

Time to get away then, but before I did, I rummaged through his pockets, took his wallets, there were a few of them and loaded them into my rucksack.

Then I ran like the wind, gripping the bleeding wound on my side.

Having never intentionally killed anyone before I woke up on Saturday morning, I had now murdered two people in the past twenty-four hours.

I headed about a mile east to be sure that I was as far away as possible from my latest crime. I found a small, rundown hotel in the Rue de Chabrol and paid sixty-five francs for one night, taking care to hold my rucksack over the bleeding wound on my side when navigating the night porter who was acting as the overnight receptionist.

The porter had asked for some proof of identity, but I had told him it had been lost on the train to Paris from Lyons. For a twenty-franc tip he had turned a blind eye. That was my eighty-five francs gone. Still at least I had some more money. I did not know how much yet.

The check-in process took longer than I hoped. It probably seemed longer than it was due to the fresh, painful knife wound I was trying to simultaneously nurse and hide. As I completed my paperwork, the porter asked me about my reason for coming to Paris.

"To get rich." I had told him.

As he insisted on slowly and arthritically taking me to my room, he shared his story about making money.

"The son of a friend of mine worked for a large middle-eastern oil company. He was sent to Saudi Arabia, business class on a plane. On the flight there was a competition that he entered."

The porter reached the first landing, took a moment to recover his breath. I tried to negotiate finding my own way to the room, but the porter seemed insistent on taking me the entire way. It was as though the story he was telling me was timed for the slow climb.

He continued.

"When my friend's son arrived in Saudi Arabia,

there was a luxury, chauffeur-driven car from his company waiting to take him to the hotel. Anyway, he arrived at the hotel and there was a message waiting for him at the reception." The porter paused for probably the least poignant dramatic effect I had experienced.

"He had won the airline competition. It was one thousand dollars. And of course…"

Please let the story end now, I thought, as the porter pulled himself up the final steps.

"He decided to give the money to his company and funnily enough, he was only there to help the company save that amount of money, so they flew him home."

My mind was doing press-ups. His story made no sense; why would any sane company send someone so far on such an expensive trip to save so little money? Why would any logical person give money they won to his employer? Why did the airline wait for him to leave the airport and arrive at the hotel before telling him he had won a competition? …

The porter placed a huge steel baton in my hand. It had two rings of soft rubber around one end.

Was this to hit him with for telling me such a terrible story?

I looked at the object and at the opposite end to the rubber rings was a small hole, a small steel ring, an engraved number, and a small steel room key.

"Remember not to take the key out of the hotel. Always leave it at the reception desk," said the porter.

There was clearly little chance of anyone sane

taking the heavily weighted key out of the hotel. The fob must have weighed a couple of kilos. I put the key in the door to my room and opened it. I took the key out, flicked on the light switch and turned to face the porter, blocking him as he tried to enter the room.

"That was certainly," I paused, "a story." *A real shit story missing all the necessary ingredients*, is what I really thought.

"You are most welcome. I hope it helps you learn something useful about getting rich," he said and then held out his hand for a further tip.

Unbelievable. He had slowed me down and told me the worst story I had ever heard, and he had done this for a tip? Little wonder he seemed to have no money.

As he stood at the door to the room with his hand held out, I contemplated pushing him backwards down the staircase. The trouble was that I had so many problems right now, I could not afford to add to them.

"Goodnight," I said, gave him one of my fake smiles and then shut the door on him. Nobody deserved money for that excuse for an anecdote.

Chapter Twenty

Once the door to the room was closed, I turned around to inspect it. Was that it? I had never seen a bulb glow so dimly. Everything had a price and I guessed that included wasting electricity. Even in this dim light it did not look like the room would benefit from more illumination. Bright light might scare the rats and cockroaches.

The room was basic. It made my bedroom at Grandmas' house seem palatial. It didn't look like the room had been painted since the French revolution. The mattress and sheets could also have come from the same time period.

I threw the rucksack on the bed, gently removed my jacket and lifted my t-shirt to examine my knife wound.

The cut was around three inches long and did not look too deep.

I needed some clean bandages but that was not an option at this time in the early morning and there was no way I could risk going into any hospital. If I went to a hospital, questions would be asked, and the police would be called. I did not have any identification. In fact, I did not really have an identity I could use either. The police might even be looking for me.

I took my already blood-stained t-shirt off, tore it into strips and wrapped the wound as best as I could.

I would get the medical supplies that I needed after some sleep.

The room had a small bathroom where it was quite possible to leave in a dirtier state than you entered.

The shower tray was brown with slime, the shower screen was covered in stains, water dripped from the tap in the sink. The bathroom light did not work, so it was only illuminated from the one ceiling lamp in the bedroom. The bathroom was too grimy to risk bathing my wound in.

I have come to find that a quick test to understand the cleanliness of any bathroom is to check the soap. Is there any? What condition is it in? Is it hygienically wrapped?

In this bathroom, there was a much-used, often ignored, cracked, dried up slither of ancient soap resting on the sink. There were streaks of grey down the cracks. Dead skin perhaps? I had to prize the soap from the sink where it had dried on the ceramic. When I flipped the soap over, there were several curly, springy hairs on the other side. It had longer pubic hair than I did. Yuk. I would not want to be rubbing that over my body, let alone over an open wound.

On the upside, the carpet in the bedroom was so filthy that if I did drip any blood, it probably would not be noticed.

I switched the single light in the room out, lay on the bed. By then, it must have been sometime after three in the morning. I did not know for certain as I had no watch and there was no clock in the room.

I just stared up at the ceiling for an exceptionally long time, contemplating my cataclysmic losses and how my life had become so entirely decimated in the course of a single day.

I finally fell asleep.

Chapter Twenty-One

I did not sleep well. The bed was even less comfortable than the passenger seat in Renaud's truck and the cut on my side would sear with pain and wake me up each time I moved.

By eight in the morning, I resolved to get what supplies I could. I started by carefully inventorying what I now had. There were Daz's clothes that I still needed to get rid of. There were some of my own clothes and the four wallets I had taken from the mugger.

The first wallet contained just eighty francs and a credit card.

The second wallet had three hundred francs, the third was the heaviest; two thousand francs. There were fewer forms of photo identification at that time, at least nothing that would fit into a wallet, so I had no idea if the person named in the fat wallet, Jean-Claude Fontaine, was the person I had killed or someone he had mugged.

The fourth and final wallet only contained some coins.

I took the money out of each one, put it in my pocket and threw the wallets into the plastic bag containing Daz's clothes. I intended to burn that bag and its contents at the earliest opportunity.

2,398 francs including the coins, plus of course, I still had £14.98 in British currency. That might last me for a month or two if I was careful.

I also found the slip of paper with Renaud's contact number in my jacket pocket. I memorized it. He was the only new contact I had so far. Once I had it stored in my head, I scrunched up the paper into a ball and put it in my pocket.

My first priority was to buy some medical supplies.

I found a small pharmacy in the same street, with a line of mopeds parked outside. I purchased plenty of bandages, antiseptic, plasters, scissors, a bar of soap, a comb and some roll-on underarm deodorant, then headed straight back to my room.

As I entered the lobby, the receptionist had changed, it was now a very disgruntled looking old lady. "Check out is at 10am," she said as I passed her desk.

In the room, I took a shower, cleaned the wound with the new bar of soap, then the antiseptic, laced the cut with plasters and then bound my middle with the bandages. I took out my final clean t-shirt and slipped it on.

My brown hair was eighties long at the time. I combed some of the water out. I had neglected to buy any hair product. No matter. I had at least seen a hair dryer in the room.

The hair dryer was old and had a short power cable. The only mirror was in the bathroom and the only power socket was on the other side of the bedroom. I plugged the hair dryer in, pulled it as far across the floor towards the bathroom as possible and then paced out the distance between the mirror and the dryer. It was about eight feet short.

I dried my hair without using the mirror and it ended up looking spectacularly frizzy.

I put the possessions I was not wearing into the rucksack, being careful to place the bag full of incriminating evidence at the top. I needed to get rid of it all as soon as possible.

When I entered the hotel, I had thought about staying for more than one night because it seemed cheaper than I had expected, but the room was so bad, I needed to find somewhere better.

I handed my key over at the desk to the tutting old lady pointing at the clock; *10:05*. There was now a young woman with the old lady. She was a slender girl of about my age or perhaps a year older, with a plastic cradle of presumably ornamental cleaning products. *Perhaps the world's worst cleaner?* I thought.

The younger girl smiled at me. Was that a flirty smile? I did my best to fake a smile in return only to see her face move instantly from allure to … was that pity? What had gone wrong?

I turned around and saw a mirror behind me. I repeated my smile. Cynthia would have said that at that moment, I had *hair like a mad woman's fanny*. When I smiled, my crooked teeth appeared. The ensemble of the hair and the teeth was quite… striking. And not in a good way.

I resolved to put together a list of my personal priorities; Buy clothes, get a new identity, work out how to make more money and of course *get my teeth straightened.*

Breakfast at the café on the corner was the first time I felt I had been able to relax in a while. The orange juice and the croissant were much fresher than anything I had experienced living with Grandma.

The café had a small selection of newspapers in a rack for paying customers to browse. They were all French newspapers. I looked at the dates. None of them were from today. I picked up one anyway.

I had a realization that I had perhaps identified the fifth rule of getting rich; *be ruthless and bold.*

If I had not been, I would now be locked up in a jail back in England or a dead stab victim down a Parisienne side street or perhaps just completely penniless. My recent actions had not made me rich, but they had certainly put me into a better position to achieve my ultimate goal.

From my brief foray to the pharmacy, I had noticed most shops were closed. I had put that down to the time of day, but now it was mid-morning, and I was on the main road lined with shops I could see that they were all closed. Sunday.

As I glanced through the out-of-date newspaper, I noticed one item of interest; Mr Pierre Deveraux was scheduled to attend a book signing at the Librarie Galignani in the Rue de Rivoli at 2pm on Tuesday. That might be a good opportunity to finally meet this potential role model.

I ordered another orange juice and croissant and

sat at a table on the edge of the café. The table and chairs were on the pavement, and I had placed my rucksack on the chair opposite me, perhaps because disposing of the contents was one of the many problems I was contemplating.

Where was I going to be able to live? How would I earn money? How would I get a new identity? What new identity should it be? And how on earth was I going to get rid of a rucksack full of incriminating evidence?

At least on the financial side, I knew I was okay for a short time. When it came down to earning more money, I considered mugging. However, mugging seemed to be a dangerous activity. After all, the first mugging I had witnessed in Paris had ended with the death of the assailant.

It was at that point that I thought about the Aikido advice, *blend with the river.*

When it came to the biggest river of money I knew about in Paris, it all belonged to Pierre Deveraux. Maybe where I was going wrong in my attempts to get rich was trying to make my own money from scratch. Perhaps what I needed to do instead was to usurp someone else's river of money. Nobody I knew about had more wealth than Pierre.

A takeover. I would work out how to take over ownership and control of Pierre Deveraux's business empire… and maybe, if Renaud was to be believed, I would take over his criminal empire too.

It was just as I sat back contemplating this new objective and sipping my second orange juice that I got mugged for a second time. This time, things went far more smoothly… for the mugger.

A young man grabbed the rucksack from the chair opposite and fled to the pillion position of a waiting moped. They moved away at low speed with the tiny engine straining under the weight of the two riders.

I calmly downed the remainder of my orange juice.

I had momentarily considered trying to prevent the theft, but my public situation had pushed me towards inaction. If I tried to stop them on a crowded street and was successful, the Gendarme would be called. I would be noticed.

Besides, there was no chance of burning a rucksack in central Paris without it being noticed. All my money was in my pocket. Having the rucksack taken was one less thing that I needed to immediately worry about.

Nobody noticed the theft apart from me. But I needed to disappear before the thieves opened the bag. They would certainly be disappointed with most of the contents; dirty underwear and assorted items of blood-soaked clothing. They might get to the wallets and credit card I had left but equally they might not get down that far. They might come back and throw the contents at me. They might even know the mugger I had killed, and his credit card might be the one in the bag.

At the very least, the thieves should figure out that I was guilty of something. They probably would not be able to recall my face at this point, but they certainly would if they came back.

I needed to get off the street.

I paid my bill, got up and walked back to the Hotel. On the short route back, I found a bin and put the ball of paper with Renaud's number in it.

I negotiated a discount to stay for one month for twelve-hundred francs, acquired the caddy of second-rate cleaning goods and went back to the room and began to scrub.

Chapter Twenty-Two

Cleaning the hotel room was therapeutic. I was careful not to exert my wound. I probably could not buy more clothes until tomorrow and this activity had many benefits, not least being that I would have a clean room at the end of the process.

I would occasionally head down to reception to borrow items, a vacuum cleaner, a bucket and a step ladder.

The girl from reception came to my room to look at the work I was doing.

"Don't worry I am not trying to steal your job,'" I said.

She was not worried. It turned out that she was the daughter of the receptionist and the night porter, a couple it seemed, whose relationship worked very well when they only saw each other briefly at each shift change.

"I am Francine," she said.

What name had I used at reception?

"Eugène."

Given the state of my appearance, I did not think Francine was hitting on me. I suspected she was bored and trying to avoid accidentally making any of the rooms acceptably clean.

"What bought you to Paris?"

"A train."

"No, I meant, why have you come here. You

don't seem to know anyone."

"There was a death in the family."

"Oh. So, you are here for the funeral?"

"Yes." In a way this was true. I was here avoiding the funeral, especially the one in which I was supposed to be in the coffin.

Francine told me a bit about her parents, Maurice and Madeleine. Her mother had come from a wealthy family but now they only had the run-down hotel to show for it.

The hotel had forty-eight rooms and on a typical evening only a small number of them were occupied. Guests rarely stayed more than one night and sometimes, even a single night was a stretch goal.

I asked if her parents had considered improving the hotel?

According to Francine, her parents were short of money. They could not even afford to hire any staff and with just the three of them and what she referred to as *expensive local taxes*, they never managed to do anything more than scrape by.

As I continued to clean the room, Francine decided it was time she moved on.

"Would you like to borrow my radio?"

"That would be great," I had said. A radio would be good for two reasons. Firstly, my French was a little rusty but secondly because I was keen to hear a current news programme. I did not tell Francine these things.

Minutes later she appeared with an old radio which she plugged into the one power socket in the room. I thanked her and she left, reappearing intermittently to check on my progress and borrow back various cleaning items to continue her own work.

After searching through the radio stations, I found one which was mostly phone-in discussions from the public about *le situation en France a present.*

At one o'clock in the afternoon, I finally got to hear a news bulletin.

The lead story was about a heightened state of terror alert, especially in Paris, due to a recent series of bombings.

In a potentially unrelated incident, a man had been found dead in the ninth arondissement in the early hours of the morning. Police were appealing for witnesses. *Should I come forward?* I don't think so.

And then came the news I had been waiting for:

Police in England have launched a manhunt for a sixteen-year-old British boy following a double-homicide in the southeast of the country yesterday. Darren Pearson, or Daz as he was known is believed to have fled after bludgeoning two victims and then setting fire to their house. The names of the victims are not being released until police have managed to track down and notify their next of kin.

Next of kin. The words sounded empty. Grandma and I had no next of kin. Somewhere there was my mother but good luck finding her. The Gendarme never did after my father died.

A thought struck me, and I added *find my mother* to my list of things to do.

The British police appeared to have taken the bait

that I had left and were only looking for Darren. This was excellent news.

By the time I had washed the walls, scrubbed the skirting boards, cleaned the shower, the sink, the toilet seat, vacuumed the floor and even wiped the lightbulb clean of dust, it was just gone seven o'clock.

I stepped back to admire my work. It looked like a different room. Still shabby, but clean shabby.

I had skipped lunch for fear of accidentally being located by the people that had stolen my rucksack earlier. I didn't want them demanding a refund or trying to extort money from me due to the contents it had.

The seven o'clock news bulletin alleviated my immediate concern:

A pair of moped thieves have been caught and charged with the murder of twenty-two-year-old Jean-Claude Fontaine. They were found in possession of Mr Fontaine's wallet, together with several items of blood-stained clothing.

Time to find something to eat then.

I made a series of trips down to the lobby with the bucket, ladder, vacuum cleaner and cleaning caddy. It was nearly time for the shift change and Maurice, Madeleine and Francine decided to collectively come upstairs to inspect my handywork.

They were impressed. Madeleine was full of recriminations suggesting Francine should be able to get every room up to this standard. Maurice defended her. *Forty-eight rooms and this took a young and fit man about nine-hours to do just one.*

Maurice hit upon the idea of offering me one

week of free accommodation for each room I cleaned to this standard. I told him I would keep that offer under consideration.

As we all headed back down to the small reception area on the ground floor, there were three men waiting for Maurice.

"These are the expensive local taxes," Francine said quietly under her breath to me.

This was not my battle, and I could not afford to get into any more trouble. Besides, there were three of them and they were each considerably larger than I.

As I walked slowly past them, I saw Maurice open a cash tin and pass across a clutch of bank notes.

I waited outside the hotel. A few minutes later, the three men emerged.

"Excuse me." I said in my best Parisienne accent.

The largest and oldest of the three men stopped the group and threw me a menacing stare; "What do you want…" He paused and looked me up and down, then added, "boy?"

I realized I was giving him my normal neutral stare. I changed it to the best fake smile I could muster.

"A job," I said.

Chapter Twenty-Three

Be innovative. That is get rich rule number six. Whereas invention is the art of turning ideas into reality *using* money; innovation is about using opportunities in novel ways to *create* money.

Most people would have seen the presence of three threatening men taking money as something to avoid, but I needed to know a lot more about crime. I needed to know more about how to do it. I also needed to understand how powerful Pierre Deveraux was. Did he control the Parisienne criminal underworld?

These were the days before the Internet when the only way to acquire knowledge was to find it out, either from a book or someone that knew what they were talking about. Unfortunately, there is a lot of information that never gets into books. There are also many people who assert they can provide accurate knowledge about topics when in fact they cannot.

If I wanted to know about crime and making money, then I needed to get close to genuine experts on these topics.

Although I knew a fair amount about how to fight, it seemed that I had barely scraped a victory in my last encounter. I needed to improve that skill, I also needed to know who not to fight and I needed to earn money.

It was impulsive, but I thought all of these things would probably be considerably easier if I joined a gang of criminals.

Blend with the river as my Sensei had instructed me.

There was also the strong possibility that if I needed a set of new identities, these people would be sufficiently connected to know how and where I could obtain reliable, fake papers.

By the following morning, I was an apprentice member of a criminal gang. Unlike other forms of employment, there were absolutely no references required for this role and no proof of identity needed either.

The initial hours of work would mainly be late at night, and I took the opportunity to start a process of transformation.

I visited a coiffeur to get my hair cut short and bleached blonde.

I visited an optician and acquired a set of glasses. I didn't need them; they were plain glass, but I had explained to the salesperson that I just wanted them so that I could look more intelligent. The optician had looked back at me as though my request was a contradiction to my assertion. It did not really matter what he thought, only that I acquired the glasses.

I had no intention of wearing these glasses during my criminal activities, these would be for my second persona.

I went to the Boulevard Haussmann and purchased some new clothes, underwear, shoes, trainers, toiletries, a radio for the room, a pen, some razor blades, some pins, a length of chain and a new rucksack.

Of all the items I purchased, the only one to raise an eyebrow were the razor blades, perhaps because with my smooth skin I did not look like I needed to shave yet. I had pointed at my armpits, then used the fingers of my hand to indicate too much hair sprouting from them. That was uncomfortable enough for the lady serving at the till to want to finish the transaction swiftly.

As Jake had unintentionally taught me; if you make a situation uncomfortable enough, then people prefer to swiftly move on.

By the time I arrived back at the hotel that evening, I looked so distinctively different that Madeleine did not recognize me at first. She stopped me at reception and asked where I was going.

"New haircut," I said. She looked taken aback.

"It's very…er… nice," she said politely and handed over the huge steel baton with my tiny room key on the end.

The haircut was not nice, I looked like a reject wannabe version of Val Kilmer (the *Top Gun* hair), but no matter. The important thing was that I looked nothing like Henri Jones, apart from the teeth.

Chapter Twenty-Four

The following day I took myself to the Librarie Galignani in the first arondissement. My own copy of Pierre Deveraux's autobiography was back in Folkestone and potentially burnt to a crisp by this point.

There were copies stacked high of his autobiography, all of them were the more expensive hardback edition and all of them were the original French version.

I picked one up from the pile and joined the long queue for it to be signed.

As I approached the desk, I could see Monsieur Deveraux in real life for the first time. He was a lean and tidy man in his early sixties, with a flash of silver hair and an expensive suit. On either side, he was flanked by two heavily built but smartly dressed men, undoubtedly some personal security contingent. Immediately to his left and right behind the desk were two female assistants, one diligently opening each copy to the page for signing and the other lifting each signed book away.

The signing seemed perfunctory. He would look up, ask who it was for, sign it and then it would be taken from him and replaced with the next.

When I finally reached him, I seized my opportunity to ask him one question.

"Who is this for?" he asked.

"I am probably your greatest fan," I said, but I have to confess that sentiment was probably not conveyed by my very unemotional and neutral demeanour.

He sighed.

I proceeded to ask my question; "Mr Deveraux. Can I ask, what would you say was the most important rule to follow if you want to get rich?"

"Be resourceful," was his reply. *"Don't think exclusively about what you think you have, look to acquire and leverage what you need."*

With that, the book was signed and passed back to me by his assistant. As I turned around, I heard a click and I saw another of his entourage take a picture. I had not seen them take a picture of anyone else. No matter. I just hoped it would not appear in any newspaper. There was nothing I could do about it now.

As I moved away, I opened the book to the signature page. In it he had inscribed:

To my greatest fan. Be resourceful. Pierre Deveraux.

That is in my opinion the seventh and final rule for getting rich: *Be resourceful. Do not be constrained to only think about what you have; work out what you need and get hold of it.*

I was pleased with my new book. It was a book I had already read a couple of times in English, but now I had a signed edition in French, with some great advice from the person I wanted to take everything from.

I also managed to buy an English newspaper; *The*

Times, a copy from the previous day which contained some more information about the double-murder in Folkestone. The manhunt for Darren in the UK was in full swing.

I wondered about Mr Canning. He was the only person that would know I was still alive. *Would he do anything to alert the police to what really happened? Could he do anything more? Would he think he had already done enough to ruin my life?*

Chapter Twenty-Five

To my new criminal friends, I decided to keep my ability to speak English a secret.

Victor, Felix and Gustave were my new mentors. They liked having an apprentice in the gang.

They were similarly taken aback at my fresh look; Felix had asked if I painted my toenails as well. Victor remarked that he hoped I was not as stupid as my feet.

Victor was the oldest and most senior of the three. He had a face that looked like it had received a fair number of punches in its time. He was probably in his early forties, covered in tattoos and missing three fingers on his left hand.

Felix and Gustave were younger, late twenties maybe and with slightly less tattoos. Felix also had one finger missing, the little finger. His missing finger was on his left hand too.

They had asked a bit about me. I was Eugene LeBeau, a sixteen-year-old orphan from Lyons who had runaway to Paris to seek a better life. As *Le Beau* was French for *the beautiful*, they found my last name amusing.

"My friend; Beautiful you are not," Victor had said "Especially now that you look like a match that has been dunked in correction fluid."

But maybe if you get me some tattoos and break my nose in a few places like the rest of you, that will help improve my looks. I thought this but dare not say it aloud because that is exactly what they would have done purely for the fun of it.

There was no way I wanted any tattoos. It would be a distinguishing mark that would make it hard to swap identities effectively if and when I needed to.

I was also intrigued and concerned about how two of them had managed to lose fingers. I was quite attached to my own fingers and was keen that they remain on my hands.

The first skill they needed to ascertain was if I could fight and how well. I was not keen to reveal my true competence in this area in case I needed that as an element of surprise sometime in the future. However, it seemed reasonable that they wanted to know if I could give and receive a good, hard punch.

They took me to a small park. Victor and Gustave sat on a bench and left Felix to run me through the basics. I had to punch his hand. He had to punch my hand. I had to dodge a punch. Then I needed to see if I could wrestle Felix to the ground. Felix was far heavier than I. Perhaps I could have done it, but I was not going to. I was here to learn, not to teach.

"You punch like a girl," Felix had said and then showed me how to punch harder. It was actually him who had the weak punch, but I let him think I was impressed with his strength and that I was showing him the limits of my own.

Next up was Gustave. He was larger again and showed me his defensive moves and blocks.

Finally, there was Victor, who was built like a

munitions bunker. His punch was something to be reckoned with and I was sure that nothing short of an explosion could knock him off his feet.

"Okay. Do your best to hit me." Victor held the top of my head at arm's length and the other two laughed as his reach prevented me from landing any punches. I did not like being humiliated, so I grabbed the hand he was using to hold me with both of my own and then swung a soft kick at his face, being careful not to put any force into it.

There was some synchronized raising of eyebrows across the team at this move. Victor concluded that I was better at fighting than he had hoped but still had a long way to go.

"How did you learn to give and take a punch?" he asked.

"I had a very charitable father. He was very generous…" I lifted my hands "…with his fists."

"Where is he now?"

"He had an unfortunate disagreement with the Paris Metro system. It was many years ago."

The second skill they taught me was how to break into places. The most important rule was this; *don't get caught.*

If you were caught, do not give the police any useful information and certainly never admit to anything.

Victor then gave me the lecture on the gang rules. Criminals had rules?

"This organization is bigger than just our gang and anybody who talks to the police, well, let's just say that they don't get to talk to anyone else after that. And if you have a family then neither do they."

"Also, once you are in the gang you cannot choose to leave. The punishment for trying to leave is the same as if you try and cheat by taking more of the money than you are entitled to."

Victor and Felix looked at each other. It told me that there was something that had not been said.

I ventured a question; "Have any of you ever tried to leave?" I wondered what the punishment was for that, but I dare not ask directly in case it made me look uncommitted.

Victor held up the one finger on his left hand and Felix held up three fingers and they both waggled them.

"So, you have tried to leave once, and Felix has tried to leave three times?"

Felix let out a short laugh and said, "You are looking at the wrong fingers."

It was then I noticed that Victor was waggling three stumps and Felix just the one where they used to have fingers.

"Only Gustave has not tried to leave or skim the gang…so far."

Gustave rubbed his full hand of fingers preciously and with apprehension.

They were all keen to move the conversation along.

"So, who runs the gang? Is it Pierre Deveraux?"

Felix, Gustave and Victor all looked at me. There was an uncomfortable pause before Victor answered.

"Monsieur Deveraux? Maybe. Who knows? But I can tell you this; It is extremely dangerous to speculate, and you should never do that again, not with us and especially not with anyone else. But I think whoever it is has nothing to do with anyone in the lower ranks."

There was yet another pause. Felix looked to Victor; "Should we tell him about the black teams?"

Victor sighed, "He will find out."

"Oh, come on," I said, "You can't mention something like that and then not give me the rest."

Victor looked at me. "You will see. But like us, you will not talk about them."

With that, the conversation was moved back to the fine art of burglary.

Just like getting rich, the first step to any break-in was research and reconnaissance. Indeed, I was breaking in to the Parisienne criminal underworld using exactly the same tactics.

"We need to go and meet a man to help us with the break-in for tomorrow night."

Chapter Twenty-Six

Victor, Gustave, Felix and I walked to a bar in a back street near the Gare Du Nord, the northern railway station in Paris. The place was filled with smoke. Whoever inadvisably carpeted the place had at least had the sense to never bother to clean it. My shoes stuck to what I presumed from the smell was old, decaying spillages of beer and wine. The thin layer of discarded cigarette ash coating the carpet seemed to be working like a reverse version of grit on snow; allowing shoes to get some degree of freedom from the extraordinarily tacky surface.

"Over there." Victor pointed at a huge, muscular brute standing at the bar, carrying even more tattoos than our entire team.

"What is it with criminals insisting on getting tattoos?" I didn't mean to say this aloud, but I must have done because Victor replied.

"He isn't a criminal. He's the security guard at the place we are going to rob."

Felix smiled, "He is kind of a criminal. But then many security guards would argue that the exceptionally low wages for security guards are also criminal."

Victor greeted the man with vigour and embraced him at the shoulder. "Bouzile" said Victor.

Was that his name?

"Bousiller?" I asked. It was odd because I knew

this to be the French word for screwing things up. It did not fill me with confidence.

"It's the name of the small village in Western France where I was conceived," Victor's friend replied. He seemed slightly angry at my comment. He probably received the same observation all the time, but if so, surely the thing to do would be to change his name.

His parents were clearly not geniuses, but then, evidently, neither was he.

I made a mental note that probably only stupid people name children after the place of conception.

Bouzile signalled for us to go to a corner table, which was quickly vacated by the people sat there once this huge man and our gang appeared.

There were only four seats at the booth, so I was left to stand up at the end of the table like a low-budget minder. This seemed to please Bouzile.

"What's with the new manbaby?" I presumed Victors' friend was referring to me. How rude.

Victor looked over to me; "Gene. Go and grab two bottles of red wine. Tell Emile to put it on my tab."

Something sparked in my mind. I had been thinking about how objectionable Victor's inside man seemed to be… but that name. *Emile*. Surely it could not be the same Emile. The tubby, grubby smelly man my mother had run off with. Surely, I would already have noticed if it were.

The last time I had seen Emile was eight years ago. I was considerably shorter then. Maybe I had missed noticing him. But I had not seen a tubby, grubby barman. Just a slim, clean shaven, middle-aged bartender.

I spun around to hide any reaction.

I wandered towards the busy bar. A better bar might have had table service, but this place was packed, messy and understaffed.

The bartender was working his way down the customers, juggling his tasks, pouring beer, decanting wine and occasionally responding to the *ting* of the kitchen bell by recovering food from a hatch and ungraciously placing it in front of the relevant customer, or calling them over to the bar.

This man was slimmer than my Emile, but there was something familiar about his face.

As I waited my turn at the bar and contemplated the barman's identity, I looked down the row of people.

There was another face I recognized. *How could I recognize a face in a Paris bar? I had only been back in Paris for less than a week.*

Where did I know that face from?

Hell's teeth. It clicked. That was Detective Constable Ross.

I pulled back slightly from the bar to take my own face out of view. What the fondue was he doing here? Had they tracked me down? Were they looking for me? Why was a British police officer at a bar in Paris?

The pieces clicked together quickly. The bartender must be Emile, my Emile. The police would be searching for Henri Jones' mother and hopefully not for Henri Jones. They needed to inform her about Henri's death.

I had no idea if it was usual to send a British Police officer over. Would Detective Ross recognize me? It was about five years since I had last seen him or Carl. My hair colour was different from the Henri Jones he had known. Would that be different enough?

My other thought was - *Wow, Emile really got his act together. Almost.* He still worked a bar, but boy did he look better than I remembered. The Emile I knew had no concept about personal grooming or diet. I guessed that might have been my mother's influence. I mean Henri's mothers' influence.

I had to remember; Henri is dead. I had not worked out who I was going to be yet, but it certainly was not someone with Henri's back story.

Could Detective Ross speak French? I doubted it. I leaned forward and glanced at the people either side of him. The man on his right looked too smart and clean for this bar. Probably a member of the local Gendarme.

Sure enough, as Emile reached the two men, the man I suspected was a French police officer flashed some identification and started to talk with Emile for longer than a drinks order.

Emile was animatedly pointing at the busy bar. There was nobody apart from him and whoever was in the kitchen. He seemed to be looking at his watch and putting up some protest.

The discussion became more heated. There was a lot of shrugging from Emile. Detective Ross seemed focused on the conversation his colleague was having with Emile.

Eventually, Emile ushered the men behind the bar and into the kitchen, whilst he carried on serving.

Emile chimed a spoon against a glass and broadcast to the bar that there would be a short delay to any existing food orders and no new orders for now. The hubbub that had quietened down quickly livened up again and Emile continued working his way down the bar through the drink orders.

When he reached me, I ordered the wine to Victor's tab and took the bottle and glasses over to the table in two trips.

"What was that about?" asked Victor.

"Police in the kitchen," I replied. Victor and the others shuffled uncomfortably in their seats and looked around.

"How many?" asked Victor.

"Two, I think. Not in uniform."

"Not a raid or an arrest then," Victor concluded. "They would have at least ten men if it was anything to do with us."

Felix suggested it was probably for the series of crimes the bar had made against French cuisine. "Have you tried the French Onion Soup here? Burnt *and* cold."

"Just like my grandmother used to make," I added. His description had reminded me of her own culinary abuse. Nobody got the reference.

After the others had poured themselves a generous glass each, we were already on to the second bottle. I picked up my drink and suggested that as there was no seat for me, I would go back up to the bar.

I found a stool and then focused my attention through the kitchen hatch. I tried my best to filter out the general hubbub in the bar and to listen to what was being said. It was not possible to hear anything, but I could see them standing and talking to a lady. I could not see any of their faces.

Was it my mother in there? Almost certainly it was.

Whatever was said did not seem to have a tangible impact on her. I could see no change in body language. There was no slumping, no tears, no closing in of the two police officers to console her.

I watched them for about ten minutes before Gustave made an appearance next to me.

"We have decided that for this job you will drive the getaway car."

There was one issue with that. "It's a great idea, but I have not learnt to drive yet," I said.

Gustave contemplated my response for a moment and then quipped "It's Paris. You should fit right in with the other drivers." Then he paused. "Okay, so tonight we steal a car and teach you."

I was always up for acquiring a new skill. Learning to steal a car and then learning to drive one seemed like an excellent two-for-one deal. A steal one, get one free offer.

"That sounds like a very good idea," I said.

My focus had been distracted and I had not noticed the two policemen finish their conversation and re-emerge from the kitchen to the bar.

"Henri?" boomed a very British voice.

I looked around. Detective Ross was stood a few feet from me on the other side of the bar. Oh crap.

There are moments in life when you just have to play the cards you have and hope for the best. I ignored the call and turned to continue a conversation with Gustave.

"Henri?" Detective Ross leaned across the bar and prodded me hard on the shoulder. I mustered my strongest Parisienne accent, "Par-don?"

"Are you Henri Jones?"

I shot him a confused look and replied "Je ne comprende pas. Parlez-vous Francais?" (I don't understand. Do you speak French.) I was reasonably sure he spoke no French.

"Just wait there," he said in English and called his colleague over. They spoke together for a minute, as Detective Ross pointed at me repeatedly. I contemplated running but realized that would be a mistake. The ruse would be over and a massive manhunt for Henri Jones would begin right there in Paris.

"What's that about?" asked Gustave quietly.

"Erm." I had to think quickly. "Gustave, if they ask, you have known me for 2 years and remember, my name is Gene, and I am 18."

I barely got the words out before the French

police officer approached me.

"Bonjour Monsieur." said his Gendarme colleague – and then continued in French, "My British colleague and I are officers of the law. He has noticed that you have a striking resemblance to a person of interest in a murder enquiry…"

I could see both of Gustave's eyebrows temporarily twitch.

"Do you have any identity papers on you?"

"Here? No. Who does he think I am?" I asked.

"Henri Jones."

"My name is Gene, and this is my friend Gustave."

The gendarme looked at Gustave.

"What does this Henri Jones look like?" asked Gustave. "He must be very unusual to make the same fashion mistakes as Gene."

The gendarme did not answer Gustave's question and instead added one of his own to Gustave.

"How long have you known each other?"

"Oh. Let me think now." Gustave played the part brilliantly. He looked up as though trying to remember. "About two years ago when he was 16."

The gendarme then looked at me; "So you are not Henri Jones?"

"Who is Henri Jones?" Gustave asked the officer.

"He was thought to be a murder victim in Great Britain, but my colleague seems to think your friend looks a little like him."

"Oh." said Gustave. "So, Gene looks like a British corpse. I am sure we will have fun ribbing him about that for many years to come." He fake belly-laughed at his own joke and then added, "We have always said he looks a little too pale."

With that he grabbed me and marched me out of the bar. We didn't stop to talk with the others.

Once outside the bar, Gustave encouraged me to run with him and we made our way to another bar several streets away.

On the way, Gustave made the comment. "So, you are a British murderer. It can be our little secret but remember that you owe me one."

I didn't bother to deny it. Perhaps I should have, but I was grateful for getting out of the immediate situation.

"Won't they look for me now?"

"I don't think so," said Gustave. "I remember what you looked like a few days ago and now I understand this transformation. All they know is that they saw someone who looks very slightly like someone who is supposed to be dead. What were they doing there?"

I lied. "I have no idea." What else could I do? Tell Gustave that we accidentally ended up at a bar where my estranged mother now lived with the bartender?

Gustave had the decency not to ask any more questions, at least not at that point, although maybe that was because he thought he would not get honest answers.

Chapter Twenty-Seven

"To summarise then. It turns out that Gene," Gustave pointed at me and paused for effect, *"is a murderer."*

So much for Gustave keeping this as our little secret.

It was an hour since the incident at Emile's Gare Du Nord bar. The street outside was quiet and dark, punctuated by pools of light from occasional streetlamps and from the internal illumination emanating from the new bar we were in.

It had been raining, but it had stopped now. The surface of the street was glistening and as I stared out of the window, I could see the few lights reflected in the pools of water that collected where the road and pavement were uneven. It was now just after 1am.

Gustave, Felix and Victor were now sat with me at the new bar. Felix and Victor had seen our hasty departure and had followed at a safe distance, after first ensuring that the police had not given chase. The police were still in the bar when we left, and no police cars had come screaming around the area with sirens blaring.

I had a steel barrelled pen in my coat pocket. I was reasonably sure that I could kill Gustave if I took him by surprise and plunged the pen into his chest, but it was too late now. I would have to kill all three of them and that was unlikely to be possible. Even if I could do it, where would I go then? Probably straight to a French prison, followed by a British one.

"Worse than that," said Felix with a very serious face; "It seems Gene could be British."

All three of them faked their best shudder, as though someone had walked over their graves. They each took a sip of beer as though it was some sort of brain lubricant.

Each of us seemed to be staring off into space considering different components of the recent event. I wondered if they were considering murdering me.

"And let's not forget, he cannot drive," added Gustave.

Victor looked straight at me. "Is there anything else we should know? For example, are you also sleeping with my daughter?"

I looked back at him; "I don't know yet. Is she attractive?"

Victor laughed, "Not really. Unfortunately, she looks like her mother."

The three of them laughed.

"You see," said Victor "murder is a little bit outside *our* regular line of work." Victor took another mouthful of his beer, then added; "Was it just one murder?"

I levelled out my palm and waggled the thumb and little finger up and down, as though the middle finger was a fulcrum. It was a gesture to indicate that *one murder* was in the right ballpark. My expression was as neutral as ever.

"Wow." Said Felix. "Maybe it would be useful to

have a murderer on the team?"

They each took a further mouthful of beer. I left mine on the table.

"What I don't understand is what a British policeman was doing at that bar." Victor looked at me. "You are going to have to tell us why that was if you want us to consider letting you stay on."

I could understand the reasons they would want to know. I would insist on knowing if I was in their position. I could lie but it was starting to feel cathartic to be able to tell someone something about the real me. Perhaps it was the wine from earlier. Drinking alcohol was not a regular experience for me.

"Over eight years ago, my French mother ran away with a French barman… Emile. I had no idea they were still in Paris, let alone at that bar."

"So, Bridgette is your mother?"

Victor's question was surprising to me.

I should have dressed up the tone of my next statement. It came out like a suspicious, flat and cold observation; "You know my mother?"

He did know her. But only very vaguely and mostly due to that bar being one of a few where he had a tab running. The question remained; *What were the Police doing there?*

"I think the Police were there to notify my mother about my er… death."

Victor rubbed his brow. "Your death? Surely you would not be here if you were dead."

I stopped momentarily to consider how to most

expediently explain the situation, then said; "There was this other person who tried to frame me for a murder. I murdered him and made it look like he was me. So now they think I am dead, and they are chasing him."

"But he is dead?" asked Gustave.

I decided this was close enough to the truth. "I would say that between the caved-in skull and the fiery inferno that followed, his recovery would be extremely… unlikely."

"And who else have you murdered?" Victor was trying to get the bigger picture.

"Opinion varies," I conceded, "I definitely did not murder my grandmother."

There was a look of incredulity around the table.

Felix was the first to react; "I am not even sure there is a name for that?"

"Grand matricide maybe? Like I said – I did not murder my grandmother. I am not a monster."

Felix took another sip of his beer.

"I am pretty sure I did not murder my twin brother."

Felix spat out his beer. I think it was more for effect, but I did notice that the look of uncertainty deepened around the table, so I added; "I was only two years old at the time."

It looked as though that seemed acceptable. "But I was the only other person in the room when he suffocated."

One step forward, two steps back. They looked unconvinced again.

Despite their reactions, there was definitely something liberating about this conversation. Years later, I would learn that many people would have called this an intervention.

"There was this mugger…" I started to add. Victor interrupted.

"Gene. I will say this only once. No more killing. If you agree not to kill anyone else, for now at least, and certainly not any of us three, then you can stay."

I was grateful. "Thanks"

There are some moments that change your life forever. This was about to be one of them. If things had gone differently right there and then, who knows what I might have become? Perhaps I would have killed far fewer people? Perhaps I would have reformed? Maybe I would have meaningfully reconnected at some point with my mother? But then it happened.

Gustave interrupted the sense of relief. He was doing that thing again, rubbing his fingers nervously. "Victor, you know this cannot be our decision. We will have to refer it to the department."

Victor straightened up his body position, as though he had become instantly sober from the beer and wine. He pulled his top lip down with his bottom lip. Then he said, with a mixture of reluctance and acceptance.

"Yes, of course."

I thought I saw Felix gulp.

If it had not already been clear to me that Gustave was a lightweight, suck-up, it was now. The stroking of the fingers, clearly whoever *the department* was ran the gangs and the discipline. It still begged me to ask the question of the others, so I did ask the question:

"Who are the department?"

Victor seemed hesitant to say anything further at this point, but he did say; "They are the people I have to go and call."

He stood up and made his way to a payphone at the back of the bar.

Gustave supped his beer as though I had not even asked the question.

Felix seemed keen to give me something; "Let's just say we are part of the unofficial layer of crime in Paris and the department, I should say Department 7, they are the official layer."

Gustave shot Felix a look and pointed to the finger on his own hand that was missing on Felix.

I could have run. Maybe I should have run. I was tired. I felt beaten. The police were on my trail, the cut on my side was still hurting. I was not used to drinking wine and beer. Victor and Felix seemed to be the closest thing I had to friends. Gustave needed to go though. Why didn't I stab him earlier?

I sat back and drank my beer.

Ten minutes later, a black Mercedes Box van pulled up outside.

"This is the department," said Victor. He led me outside and once we were beyond the earshot of Gustave, he added "I'm sorry kid."

The side door on the van slid open. Apart from the driver, there was just one man in the back.

"We need all of you." The man in the back was slim and emotionless. He reminded me of…me. Victor signalled for Felix and Gustave.

The slim man had all four of us sit on the benches that ran down each length of the cargo space. There were no windows. A steel plate sectioned off the access to the driver's compartment.

The journey took less than ten minutes. We were still in central Paris, somewhere.

When I emerged from the van, we were in an internal car park. I could tell it was not underground because it lacked that giveaway fixed temperature and musky smell that underground locations have.

Victor, Felix and Gustave were taken off in a calm but not overtly friendly manner by the driver. The slim, emotionless guy escorted me with a more abrupt and frosty demeanour.

Even though he was just one person, he had an air about him that made me believe that I was in more danger here than when I woke up to find Mr Canning's arm strangling my neck.

He invited me into a small room, what I imagined a prison cell would be like. It was around six feet on each length. There was a hard bench, a sink and a toilet set into the wall. There were no linens – just one, small clean towel. There was a strip light in the ceiling, sealed in.

"You know, this is actually better than my hotel room."

I had not meant the comment to be amusing. It was an observation. The room was forensically clean, just the way I like a room to be.

The man pushing me in made a sort of grunting sound in response to my comment and then shut the reinforced door, leaving me alone in the cell.

I heard the door lock. There was no keyhole or lock visible on my side of the door and a steel seam ensured that the mortices and other mechanisms were inaccessible.

The issue nagging at my mind was the reason behind the cleanliness of the room. It was probably not because they had exceptional cleaners but perhaps more so that if any former resident was never seen again, there would be no trace of them left in the cell.

Chapter Twenty-Eight

After a few hours, I decided I should sleep if I could.

I don't know how much time passed. I tried to keep my spirits up by positively reflecting on my situation.

Deprived of natural light, unable to tell what time of day it was, imprisoned in a cold room with no entertainment, this all felt like my recent trip to watch the *Superman IV* movie.

The corridors that had led to my room were all internal. There was no window. In fact, since entering the van, I had not seen anything of the outdoors.

By the time the cell door opened, it must have been daylight, but it could easily have been early afternoon.

It was the same man who had been in the back of the van, the same one who had put me in the cell hours earlier. He placed a grey jumpsuit on the bench, a pair of socks, soft canvas shoes and beside them a plastic box.

"Change into these and place all your clothes and belongings in the box." The skinny man just stood there.

I looked at him. Was I going to get any privacy? He just looked back at me.

"You need to do it right now. If you don't, there are consequences."

I did as he asked. I tried to keep my belt and was moving to put it around the jumpsuit.

"I don't think so." Skinny man grabbed the belt from me and inspected the underside. I had taped a length of chain, two razor blades and five pins to it.

"Pathetic," he said and threw the belt in the box.

Once in the jumpsuit, socks and shoes he motioned for me to leave the room and left the box of my belongings in the cell.

After he closed and locked the door, he escorted me down the corridor to a huge internal hall. It must have been thirty feet to the ceiling, thirty feet across and a hundred feet in length. At the far end, there was another door. Between me and the door on the far side were the familiar figures of Victor, Gustave and Felix.

Skinny man spoke again.

"If you want to live, you have to get to the other door. You are not permitted to kill any of these men – but anything else is okay," he paused. "Wait until I say *go*. Good luck. Or what is it you English say – *break a leg?*"

I have no idea how they had incentivized my comrades to fight me, perhaps it had something to do with losing more fingers.

I assessed the task at hand. Even with the incentive, I figured that at least Victor and Felix would put up more of a show and would likely refrain from beating me senseless. Gustave might be different though. He knew he had forced me into this situation. I had plans for him.

The skinny man walked down the large hall passing my three 'friends.'

Once he was at the other side, he turned around.

There was a voice over some speakers. It was in English and had a distinct English accent; "Are you ready Mr Jones?"

I looked around, I could see there were a few cameras in the corners and some speakers in the ceiling. Other than that, the hall was just a bare space, with some mats on the floor.

I was not ready. I was still tired. I had a slight headache from the wine. There was a cut in my side. I had no weapons. They outnumbered me. They were all bigger than me.

On the upside, they too appeared to have no weapons and they were all still wearing the clothes they had on last night. That should mean they were all tired.

The voice came over the speaker again, this time with a slight air of irritation: "Mr Jones?"

I nodded that I was ready.

"*Go,*" said skinny man.

The battle that followed was not pretty. Unlike the mess around in the park the day before, I had to summon up my full set of skills. I had to use the walls, the floor, every aikido trick I knew.

The truth is that I do not enjoy fighting. I especially do not enjoy being hit. Learning to fight reasonably well had already taken up far too much of my time growing up. What I wanted to learn was how to be mega-rich. To the best of my knowledge, if there was a Venn diagram showing the small circle of the super-rich and the more sizable circle of expert fighters, it was doubtful that there would be little if any overlap.

In the moment, there seemed to be little choice to my situation.

I was getting mightily fed up with being thrust into predicaments that were not of my choosing.

As I suspected, Victor and Felix made a good show but more or less allowed me to kick them hard whilst trying their best to land punches. I ducked, weaved, span.

I managed to knock Felix out first, using the momentum from bouncing off the wall and punching him hard across the face. He might not have been knocked out, but it was at least good enough for him to fake it.

Victor made a show of weaving around and tried his best to land some punches. If I were hit by any of them, that would probably be it for me. I kept my wits about me, blocking and kicking. I could tell Gustave was closing in behind me.

I had no choice. There was nothing small I could do to Victor to put him out of the fight. I lunged at him, grabbing his shoulders. I could hear the crunch as my head broke his nose. Victor fell to the ground as I pushed back from the shoulder grab and lunged at Gustave with both of my feet.

My feet hit Gustave squarely in the chest. He stumbled backwards. *Munetsuki*, I landed a series of powerful mid-strikes. *Kotegaeishi*, I had Gustave in a wrist lock. Snap. There was a satisfying sound as I heard his arm break.

Gustave yelped with pain. He was distracted, so I pressed the advantage and snapped his right leg. He cried out again.

I walked towards skinny man.

The voice came back over the speakers.

"Okay. Bring him to me. But teach him a lesson in humility first."

I didn't like the sound of that. Skinny man took up a fighting stance.

If I thought I knew how to fight, skinny man was about to show me that there are always people out there who can do it better.

"Try and punch me." Skinny man gestured for me to have a go at him. I really didn't want to.

Reluctantly I moved forward. Every attempt to punch or kick him he just blocked as though it was nothing. I tried to put him in a wrist lock, and he inverted the movement and before I knew it, he had kicked me in the face and had me on the ground.

He could easily have killed me, but he didn't. He let me up.

"Come on. Let's go see the boss."

I looked back at Victor, Gustave and Felix. Victor was nursing his nose. Felix had now got up and was supporting himself against the wall. Gustave was lying flat out on the ground writhing in pain.

I hoped the message was clear. Victor and Felix would be fine but Gustave, his recovery was going to take significantly longer.

Skinny man was not a conversationalist. He had demonstrated that any skills I might have to fight my way out would be futile. I guess that was the lesson in humility.

Skinny man led me through yet more corridors until we reached a different kind of door. This one looked particularly sturdy. He swiped a card and entered a pin code, and I heard some electromagnetic locks disengage.

On the other side of the door was an exceedingly small lift with some music playing in the background. We entered it. There were only two buttons, one for the floor we were on, marked *M* and another marked *O*.

The journey to *O* took longer than I expected. We were clearly passing more than one floor. As the pop tune played away softly in the background, I could hear the lyrics of the chorus "*…somebody got murdered…*"

I looked over to skinny man, but he didn't look back.

When we arrived at floor *O* I could at last see some natural light. It was an office and judging from the scenery we were at least five or six floors up.

There were very few people around and despite my unusual attire, a jumpsuit no less, the few office types that passed by paid no attention to me.

I noticed a sign on the wall "*Departement 7*" in steel lettering and what appeared to be a slogan below, in French of course, it translated to: "*Making your world safer."*

We entered a room. It had a whiteboard, a few TV screens which were switched off and four leather chairs set around a circular table. There was a single, sealed cardboard box in one corner.

"Sit" said mono-syllabic skinny man.

As I did so, a woman appeared at the doorway; "Can I get you a coffee or some water?"

After the events of the past day, this seemed like a surreal moment. Coffee was arranged and accompanied, thankfully by some biscuits.

We sat for several minutes. I started on the biscuits. There was a small selection and three of them were chocolate. I reached for one.

Skinny man hit my hand away; "Not the chocolate ones. The boss likes those."

"Really. I haven't eaten for nearly a day and the boss will begrudge me a chocolate biscuit," I said.

Skinny man just shrugged. "Trust me when I say, you really never want to eat the boss's biscuits."

I took him at his word and ate the plain ones.

Two minutes later a bald, middle-aged, businessman in a suit joined us. He sat down and slapped a small cardboard file on the desk. It had a name printed on it, *Henri Jones*.

From his voice, I could tell this was the Brit whose voice I had heard earlier in the fight room.

"So, Mr Jones. We managed to get most of your details from your fellow gang members and fill in the rest with the help of the local Police."

This did not sound like good news, and I think my

face may have shown this.

"But don't worry Mr Jones, the police work for us… Not all of them of course, just the dishonest ones. But we are not here to discuss the police. We are here to talk about you. Where do you see yourself in say five or ten years? Dead at the rate you are going. Although I must say, those were impressive moves earlier, taking down three men. And you – just sixteen. If they had been good at fighting that would have been very remarkable."

It did not seem as though he wanted any input from me with the rate at which he was rattling off his speech.

"According to your file, you are natively fluent in both English and French. Born in France, British father, now dead. A reasonable but not exceptional fighter already, judging from your earlier performance."

"Now we have a little decision for you to make. Our organization, well, let's say that we employ and train only the finest personnel to er… well. We help sort out security issues for various governments and major commercial organizations. Now some of this work is extremely easy to source, but some of it is not. Some of it requires ruthless mortals; people that are not impeded by too many ethical inhibitions."

"Let me get right to the point. You have a certain situation that is problematic for you. Here is some good news. We can make that problem go away. Frankly, that is exactly the kind of thing that we do. But it's expensive you see. Awfully expensive. Usually beyond the financial reach of someone like you."

He produced a calculator from his pocket and tapped away at several equations and made some notes in my file.

"By our estimations, it would be at least a high six figure fee, in Francs naturally, to bribe the necessary people, put the ghost of Henri Jones to rest and set you up with a new identity. Not this Eugene LeBeau though. It needs to be based on a real person."

"Anyway, I imagine that you probably don't have that sort of money. Am I right?"

I nodded once in agreement.

"Now we could offer you a trade. You would have to complete some initial training and then spend, well let's call it most of the rest of your natural life, working for us. But in return, you would get an increasingly generous income, in line with your skills and assignments, less the repayments for the costs we incur. It's a sort of bonded training programme. But there is a downside."

I think what he meant to say was that there were *more* downsides. He continued.

"We can't have failures in our training programme. You would need to get through training and if you didn't, well… We cannot afford to have any loose ends wandering around with second-rate inside knowledge about what we do, where we operate from and how we work. So, my first question to you is this, and please answer honestly; How do you feel generally about killing people? Did your recent situation upset you? Do you think you could do it again and if so, how often?"

My mind raced back to my conversation about murder with Renaud the truck driver. *99.9% of the time I am not murdering anyone.*

Were they inviting me to be an assassin? I didn't want to be an assassin. I don't really care about people, but so far, I had limited those actions to situations where I really, really needed to kill them for my own benefit.

For my own benefit. Those words echoed around my head.

There was a definite logic to the argument that any killing being offered was going to be for my own benefit. What if I refused? Surely, they would not let me go, or get captured by the police with what I already knew.

If I turned them down, it was not as though they would not have found somebody else to do the work.

I deflected to play for some more thinking time.

"What training would I get and how often would I have to er… apply the skills?"

The man seemed pleased with my response.

"I think we are going to get along just fine. Just never try and eat my chocolate biscuits. There always have to be certain ethical boundaries you know."

Chapter Twenty-Nine

At a time in my life when I should be having fun, I was being worked harder than at any previous point and all with the threat of certain death continuously looming over me.

On the first day, I was taken to a small room with a desk in it and required to sit a series of written tests. It was made clear to me that I did not want to fail these tests.

The first two papers were similar to the intelligence tests I had sat when I was eleven. The next two seemed to be trying to assess my personality and attitudes towards situations.

Unlike the tests I had sat when I was eleven, I was not given any information about the results.

I was given some more normal clothes to change into, black jeans, boots, a belt, a black t-shirt and an army watch. The jumpsuit and trainers were taken away.

They took my photo.

My cut side was noticed, and I was sent to a small, in-house, windowless infirmary where it was injected, stitched and bandaged.

Training was hard. Skinny man made it clear that under no circumstances should I ever again break any limbs of any colleague, *otherwise the same limb on you will be broken.*

At first, Department 7 wasted little time on me,

other than to make me train, run and fight available staff in their down time. I say fight, but really it was like I was a stress ball for each of them. A seemingly never-ending stream of new faces, mostly male but sometimes female, took turns in giving me cuts and bruises and demonstrating how comparatively poor my fighting skills were against these experts.

I was given a slightly larger room to sleep in, almost the same as the first but this time with a handle on the inside and some basic bedding, a sheet, a pillow and a coarse blanket.

The door was still kept locked most of the time I was in it, which was usually about six hours each day. There was no routine to my activities. I could be woken up a few hours into my sleep and put into the fight room.

I was given access to a small kitchen on floor M twice each day which was kept supplied with the bare essentials.

My belongings from the hotel showed up three days in, together with no explanation. They were in a cardboard box. It looked remarkably like the cardboard box that had been in my interview room on the first day.

I deduced that the Department had gone through all of my possessions. It did not matter, apart from the money, there was nothing of value.

After the first week, I was told I would be allowed to run outside. Perhaps I could use this chance to run off?

Skinny man took me to a room where he and

another man put a heavy rucksack on my back, then padlocked it to me. I had never seen a rucksack with steel wire running through the shoulder and belt straps before. It did not look like a one-off. This rucksack looked more like a factory-made suicide pack, and it weighed like it had a couple of concrete bricks inside.

Skinny man opened the back of it, and I heard a tick-tick-tick. Had he really put an explosive in it? It was not as though I could take a look.

"Be sure to run at least six miles. Be back within an hour and don't talk to any strange men, especially anyone in a uniform – or...*boom*," he made an explosive gesture with his hands.

"Someone will be following you." He looked into the pack and then used a voice that sounded like it was for someone else's benefit. "Someone will be following you but must remain at least fifty meters away. We have to think about health and safety should the explosive detonate accidentally. We wouldn't want to lose two staff on a training exercise."

Skinny man let me out through a side entrance in a back alley and told me to come back to the same door. I was not able to notice anyone following me.

When I arrived back some fifty minutes later, the voice on the other side refused to open it. *That's only four and a half miles. You need to run another mile and a half, and you only have ten minutes before the boom.*

I ran around the block as many times as I could and back to the door.

"*No,*" said the voice, "*you are still a few hundred meters short.*"

My shoulders sagged despondently, and I heard an alarm clock ring in the backpack before the door opened and skinny man told me he was disappointed.

The next day, skinny man made a point of showing me a real explosive device with a digital timer. He set it for one hour and five minutes. He placed that in the heavy backpack.

"The same rule as yesterday, but this time with real explosives," said skinny man.

These people were nuts.

I ran hard and made it back in time. Once I was in, to my surprise, the backpack was not removed. Just after the time expired, skinny man said, "You don't really think we would put a real explosive on you, do you?"

Maybe these people were not nuts.

The following day, there was no show of putting any explosives in my backpack, but the threat was repeated, *one hour or boom.*

I still ran hard. It took me fifty-eight minutes. When I reached the side entrance, to my surprise it swung open immediately. Two people set on me rapidly unlocking the pack. They opened a fortified hatch just inside the door, dropped the rucksack down a chute, then shut and sealed the door.

Moments later there was a loud bang. The hatch door was opened, and smoke came out.

Skinny man looked at me; "You don't think we would tell you when we put real explosives on you, do you?"

Yes. These people were, indeed, *nuts*.

Chapter Thirty

Three weeks in and my body felt like iron. That is when the jumping and gymnastic training began. The fight room was a flexible space where platforms and equipment would be assembled.

I learnt to jump across large gaps, how to fall from great heights without hurting myself by performing a parachute roll.

The platform height was gradually increased until it was eventually fifteen feet from the ground.

I was taught about the limitations of the human body.

In an emergency, with my professional training, a drop of around twenty feet would be possible, but any higher would result in severe injury, anything above around forty-five feet meant death was likely.

There were also two raised platform that would be positioned around ten feet up from the matted floor. They were initially six feet, nearly two metres apart.

I was taught how to run and jump distances, until I could get nearly a metre in on to the other platform.

Never try to jump between rooves that are more than three meters apart, I was told, *four meters is impossible, even if the other roof is lower.*

That same week, I was invited back up to floor O, accompanied again by skinny man who seemed to live somewhere on floor M with me.

We went back to the same room I had been interviewed in.

Coffee and biscuits arrived, and I diligently avoided the chocolate ones.

This time, the boss arrived with someone. It was the officer from the Gendarme that had been with Detective Ross in the bar some weeks earlier.

"Mr Jones, this is Eric." The boss always used English.

"I always wondered what his name was." I turned to skinny man, "Hello Eric."

"Very funny." said the boss in a tone that indicated he did not find it funny at all, "Not him, this nice policeman here. Eric has some news for you."

The officer sat and so did the boss.

Eric spoke, in French, "Monsieur Jones, you will be pleased to know that we have been able to verify your identity to the British Police as *Gene Blanchet*. As far as Detective Sergeant Ross is concerned — the matter is closed."

Blanchet. That was a nice touch since it translates to *blonde head of hair.*

Detective Sergeant Ross. It seemed Carl's father had been promoted in the past four years.

Eric continued; "The British police are happy that they are still seeking Mr Pearson in connection with the murder of Henri Jones and his grandmother." Then he passed across a brown envelope, got up and left.

The boss and skinny man remained behind. I

opened the wallet.

"Your new identity, Mr Jones," said the boss, "We needed someone about the same age, with little or no family. Preferably someone dead who we could resurrect here in Paris. Fortunately, the identity of your long dead twin seemed to fit the bill nicely, especially after we paid your mother a substantial bribe and convinced her to acknowledge that Xavier was actually sent for adoption rather than, well, you know."

I inspected the documents in the envelope: a passport and a French identity card, both in the name of Xavier Jones.

"We will be keeping hold of the passport until you need it. Does anyone in the UK know about your dead twin?"

I thought about it. Cynthia knew, but I was not going to reveal that. Grandma knew and she probably told people, but I never had.

"Possibly some of my grandmother's friends," I said "but it would be very plausible that she never knew Xavier was put out for adoption. Grandma never visited us in Paris. I don't think she liked my father. I am not sure she ever met my mother."

"I think we can make that work then, don't you Mr Jones?"

Chapter Thirty-One

During the first six months at Department 7, it was all about the training. It never ended. Eighteen-hour days reading, exercising and getting trained on skills from shooting handguns to knife fighting, human manipulation, forgery, lock-picking, reconnaissance, infiltration, poisons, how to fire a sniper rifle, woodland survival, desert survival, first-aid and finally, how to drive a car tactically and at speed.

From my mentor's perspective, I only *seemed* to slowly reach a passable level of competence in each discipline. This was basic training, and my skills would be enhanced as and when I needed them for particular assignments.

Lixorin was a tactical drug that I was told would be issued if and when I needed it. It was some kind of performance enhancing medication to boost stamina and mental acuity. I was issued with a small bottle with six tablets for my forestry survival weekend.

"One every eight hours," skinny man told me.

"What does it do?"

"You will see."

The drug kicked in within thirty minutes of taking it. All my senses seemed heightened; it pushed any fatigue away. I only took four of them and hid the remaining two away.

Despite the lower dosage, I found that I was able

to stay awake around the clock.

The downside came after the weekend. Twelve hours off the drug and wallop; all the fatigue and borrowed clarity were withdrawn with a vengeance.

One strange but welcome addition to my curriculum was a visit to an orthodontist. He insisted on giving me three fillings for teeth that he said were decayed and made impressions of my upper and lower teeth.

I visited again two weeks later and had very ugly braces added to my upper and lower jaws. On the upside, my teeth would soon be straight.

I noticed that once the brace was in place, in all the battles and fight practices, the opponents were always careful to avoid my teeth, something for which I was grateful.

The staff at Department 7 were universally distant. Nobody socialised with anybody else. Department 7 kept the use of names to a minimum on floor M, but floor O was different. Names were used there.

As I was to learn, Department 7 was a legitimate security business. The company even had a brochure outlining its' legitimate products and services, private armies, security details, private investigations, specialist security devices for espionage.

I knew they also had services that were not on the official brochure. I knew that they ran criminal gangs in Paris, gangs like Victors. I suspected that, for the right money, there was not much they would not do.

It seemed unlikely they needed anyone as young as me for any official duties, but my youthful age would probably work well for espionage. Who would suspect that any boy who looked maybe seventeen would be a trained operative?

I let them think I was happy with my new position. In a way I was. I was happy to have some expensive support and training, but my ultimate goal was still to get rich and if anyone was rich in this organization, I felt certain it was the owner.

The name Pierre Deveraux was never mentioned but I felt sure this was his outfit. Lixorin was perhaps the biggest clue. It was a pharmaceutical product and the bottle had carried the Deveraux Industries logo.

I could understand why an operation like this was useful to Pierre. Department 7 took a very expensive potential liability, the cost of paying and running an extensive network of mercenaries and flipped it into being a valuable asset.

Anyone running a vast number of mercenaries for his or her own benefit would look like a criminal, but anyone running a large commercial security company; that person just looks like an entrepreneur.

There were a few things amiss. It was my observation that despite the fifty or more people I had seen at various times on floor M, none of them seemed to be in training.

The knife instructor, Nina, presumably not her real name, had confirmed as much. *We usually just extend skills from ex-military types for specific missions. You must be important to someone.*

Maybe Pierre Deveraux had taken me at my word during the book signing. After all, someone took a photo there. As far as I knew I was not important to anyone.

It was early April before I was allowed to move out of floor M and into a small studio apartment nearby. My initial training was over, my braces were removed, and it was time for me to start earning the Department some money.

I was ordered to keep a low profile at my apartment. Any attempt to fraternize with any of my neighbours would result in my return to living in the small cell on floor M.

I was given a wallet with a cash machine card and told that was where I would find my earnings, minus a substantial deduction for payment back toward the training. I still had my French ID card, identifying me as Xavier Jones.

It was pleasing to find that although the apartment was small, it was incredibly clean. A small amount of clothing had been provided, always black jeans, an array of different coloured, crew-neck t-shirts and two reasonably stylish jackets.

There was a bed, a radio, fresh toiletries and most startling of all, there was a photo of me. More bizarrely, it was a photo of me with Pierre Deveraux. It was the one that had been taken at the book signing. I was looking down at my freshly acquired book and in the background, I could see Mr Deveraux was now looking up and sideways at me from behind.

This seemed to be present to convey a message, but it also seemed strange to openly show me there was a connection with Mr Deveraux. I took it to mean that the Department wanted me to know that they knew more about me than they ever let on.

The first thing I did with my newfound freedom was to find a cash machine and check what balance I had in my account.

Not much was the answer. A few thousand francs. Maybe it would increase over time?

Chapter Thirty-Two

For the most part, my assignments for Department 7 were local and made little use of the skills they had provided. I had to slip into quite a few offices late at night to obtain documents or photos of blueprints. I would work on security details where the security presence had to be low key.

I was not sent to perform any assassinations.

I had to attend floor G at the office at least five days each week. I had not known about floor G when I was in floor M. It had its' own entrance and was effectively a workout space for mercenaries. G for gymnasium was my guess.

There was a weekly fitness and skills check to ensure everyone was at the skills level they were supposed to be.

We each had a numbered locker with a key. If we had a new assignment, there would be a flag on the locker, and we had to visit a briefing room.

I was required to keep my watch on me at all times and ensure it was synchronized, to the second, with the floor G clock every day.

On occasion, assignments happened with no notice. A black car or van would appear, regardless of where I was. I suspected that my location was able to be tracked through a device in the company issued watch.

With the exception of floor O office staff, it was

strictly prohibited for any of us to fraternize or socialize inside or outside of work. This was an indiscretion that the company indicated was punishable by immediate termination.

Presumably, this was to ensure that none of the assets ever colluded in a way that could undermine the control of the organization. It also explained the reason that skinny man had never treated me any better than an animal he was raising for slaughter.

I did as I was told for six weeks and ignored the people in the building where the apartment was. There was the occasional friendly nod from a neighbour, or a friendly hello but nothing more.

Six weeks in and one of the residents, opening the door to her own apartment said something odd; "Hello Xavier. I haven't seen you for a while. How are you?"

I could not recall ever having seen her before. Doubtless this was some kind of test from the Department. I gave her a friendly nod and continued past her.

Despite the appearance of freedom, it was clear to me that I had almost none. They were tracking my location, even during my off hours.

I desperately wanted to visit my mother, but my locator would probably give the game away. I could take it off – but then they might try and randomly find me for an assignment, and I felt sure the consequences would be extreme.

It took me some time to work out how I was

going to navigate my situation. Eventually, the opportunity presented itself. I was sent on an assignment to steal documents from an office close to the Gare Du Nord.

The preparation and planning were exemplary as ever. Department 7 even provided keys to the office and a micro camera to obtain the copies of some commercial tender documents for a construction contract.

I took the liberty of scoping the area in the afternoon before the break-in.

That evening, I slipped into the office unnoticed and was quickly able to find the specific file. I took the photos. Then I slipped my watch off and hid it on the side. I left the office, locked the door, and headed through the corridors to the other side of the building. I picked the lock of another office door, moved through it, slid the window open and free climbed down the building.

Once on the ground I took care to avoid the side of the building where the black car was waiting for me. I made my way to the rear of the Emile's bar and into the kitchen.

My plan was to convince my mother to meet me near my own apartment, so that I could, perhaps, recruit her to help me. I would not have long to talk with her, and I had prepared what I thought I would need to say.

It was risky. Perhaps it was riskier for her than it would be for me, but in my mind, my mother owed me one. She had abandoned me years ago and if anyone could help me, it should be her.

When I slipped into the kitchen, I could see she was working on her own. She had her back to me. I didn't mean to startle her, but I definitely did.

"Mother," I said.

She dropped the knife she was using to cut some cucumber and turned around. It was years since I had last seen her face. She was not as old as I thought she would be. I guess that children always think adults are older than they really are.

I ran through my carefully prepared, succinct script in my mind.

"Xavier, my son. It's so good to see you. What have you done to your hair?" She rushed up and hugged me.

What?

It was true, I had kept my peroxide blonde look. But how on earth did she know me this well? She continued.

"It has been months since I last saw you. I thought you said you were going to disappear for longer. The police came. They told me that nasty English brother of yours is dead, but I don't believe it. They thought they saw him in the bar. But what are you doing here? I thought you were always going to keep away from Emile?"

It felt like a gut punch. My eyes narrowed. What did this all mean? It seemed to mean that far from being suffocated, my twin brother was very much alive. But how? Why had I never seen him? Where had he been taken? And how on Earth was Bridgette, *as I would now think of her*, still in contact with him?

I scrapped my plans to tell my mother anything about who I really was. *Nasty English brother.* She was clearly referring to me. What had I ever done?

"I was in the area. I thought I would drop by." I was improvising.

"Well, I can tell you that I have kept your ownership of the bar a secret from Emile, just as you asked. Thank you for buying it from the other landlord. But enough, you had better go. If Emile comes in, he will wonder who you are and I promised him I would never have any contact, not with you or your brother. You don't want him to know who you are or what you look like. You know he doesn't like criminals."

My face was frozen in thought, and I found myself staring into the middle distance.

"Stop staring like a cat."

With that, she ushered me out of the back door.

I have never felt like I was in less control of my life. I walked back to the location of the burglary in a daze. I was desperately trying to put the pieces together.

Xavier was alive.

Then I thought about the lady in the apartment building. The one that stopped me to say; *Xavier, I haven't seen you for a while.* I was sure I had never seen her before. I had not given my name to anyone in the building.

That must mean that I was staying in a place where Xavier had been living, carrying Xavier's identity papers, working as Xavier.

I carefully free climbed back up to the window I had opened. I made my way out of the room, locked the door behind, back into the target room. I picked up my locator watch and made my way, carefully out of the building through the planned escape route and to the waiting car.

"What took you so long?" asked skinny man.

"There were a lot of files. I had to find the right one." I handed him the micro camera.

With that, we drove off into the night.

Chapter Thirty-Three

An hour later, I was back at my apartment.

Unbelievable. I had an evil twin, and he was me.

Or I was him.

Or to be more accurate, we were both now *Xavier Jones*, but the current evidence suggested he was an even more despicable version.

This must be something that Department 7 knew all about. They had put me in his apartment.

More threads of the mystery swam through my mind; *Who had taken Xavier when we were two? How had Xavier become such a young component of Department 7? Had Bridgette and dad always been complicit with the lie that Xavier had been suffocated?*

Was this connected to the murder of my father?

Was my father actually dead?

None of it made sense. I stroked my jaw.

They had straightened my teeth.

I went to the bathroom mirror, opened my mouth, and looked at my fillings.

It had not felt as though I needed those fillings.

The realization dawned on me; *they had matched my dental records with the real Xavier Jones* – it was just like I had done with Darren Pearson, albeit using a dentist instead of a baseball bat.

This was not a good sign.

Matching our dental records was an indication that at some point, they planned to pass me off as the official Xavier and not necessarily at a time when I still had a pulse.

But why had Department 7 given me all of that training? All of that *basic* training. They must have thought that I would need to pass as Xavier when I was alive too.

It was almost certain that Xavier would have better training than I did. *They gave me enough to pass for him, but not enough to be dangerous to them.* That is what Department 7 must think.

I thought back to what I knew about identical twins. I knew there were two types: truly identical twins and mirror identical. Mirror twins had some aspects that were the opposite of each other. Since Xavier seemed to be a career criminal, it seemed logical and probable to assume we were truly identical.

I felt no pangs of brotherly love, no hidden bond. I was sure from his actions and from the conversation with *Bridgette* that he felt the same way about me.

Just as I had used Darren as a convenient patsy to take the place of my corpse in the house fire at Grandma's, Xavier must be considering something similar for me.

Perhaps that was another advantage I had over him. Maybe I think exactly like him.

Life can have some disappointments, but when you have aspirations as lofty as my own, finding out that you are not even the most successful version of yourself is a low point.

Crime might pay well for some people, but it was never going to make me a multi-millionaire.

It was time to turn my situation around.

It was time to apply the rules that would make me not just rich, but super-rich.

It was time to show them who they were really dealing with.

It was time to leave Department 7.

Henri Jones
needs YOU

Post a review and recommend this book to a friend to help *accelerate the release* of
Get Rich or Try Dying (Part Two)
Book 2 in the Ruthless Mortals Saga

Part two will be released within 6 months of reaching 100 verified Good Reads or Amazon reviews with 4.5 star or better average

ABOUT THE RUTHLESS MORTALS' SAGA

Have you ever stopped to think what makes somebody exceptional? Is it down to attributes, experience or is there something more random in the mix?

The Ruthless Mortals' Saga is about a group of people, each with experiences and attributes at the extreme edges of the human curve – whose paths are destined to connect and collide in ways that will determine the future of all humanity.

The Ruthless Mortals Saga is a single story, told across multiple books spanning a period of time from the mid-seventies until many years into the future.

Get Rich or Try Dying (part one) is the first book in the series.